Dest

JULIE GARRETT

Heartline
Books

JULIE GARRETT

'I'm a Libran with a love of order – but you'd never guess it from the state of my desk!' JULIE GARRETT confides. Julie loves dogs and music, particularly classical, which helps to shut out the world when she's writing.

A bookaholic, Julie's current house is bursting at the seams with all the novels she's picked up from book fairs. For relaxation, she likes to watch television (Friends and ER are her favourite programmes at the moment). She loves driving around the country researching backgrounds for her novels; once spending an entire day at Silverstone and also being taken round the Donnington racetrack at over one hundred miles-per-hour – a thrilling experience.

Julie is passionately interested in old houses and lucky enough to have a friend who's a property developer, so they talk 'houses' for hours on end. Her dream is to own a seaside cottage – but writing is, and always will, remain essential to her life.

chapter one

Cass Fairburn could never remember experiencing such a feeling of contentment as she had now, standing at her window and gazing out across a wide road and promenade at the river opposite. The Wendal wasn't a deep river at this point where it passed through the little Derbyshire town of Rydale Tor, it was merely a decorative addition to what was an already acknowledged beauty spot in the colourful brochures that advertised the county's 'High Peak'.

Rydale Tor, an immense sheer wall of limestone rock, was what gave the town its name. It plummeted down from its towering four hundred feet into dense trees and undergrowth that bordered the river. And hidden from view by that greenery were the scores of narrow Victorian pathways known locally as 'lovers' walks' that wended their way to its summit and a spectacular vantage point for almost the whole of Derbyshire.

Cass had grown to love the place in the months she'd been there. She seldom thought – or hankered after – her old life in Suffolk because that was behind her, and the future was what mattered – *her* future, and the future of baby Tiffany who had been born in Rydale's cottage hospital on a bleak November day last year.

Thinking back, Cass knew she'd done the right thing in coming to Derbyshire. The screenplay she'd been working on was finished now, and filming was due to start in a couple of weeks in a nearby village – Ashton-in-the-Peak. It was an exciting prospect – the thought of seeing her book

– the first one she'd ever written – come to life.

The time had been right to move on from Suffolk, and she'd done the only thing possible in coming here. Five-month-old Tiffany was a reminder, if she needed one, of the man she had loved and later lost, but strangely, Cass felt no regrets. She knew she would always love Patric Faulkner but at least she had the next best thing to Patric now – his child. A sudden surge of pride filled her as she turned to look at the baby who was asleep on the fat, comfortable couch behind her, and she marvelled still that a baby of such a tender age, could resemble so much the man who was her father.

She went over to the couch and perched on its edge. The movement made the baby stir, then open its big, long-lashed eyes and look up at her.

Cass picked Tiffany up, feeling at peace with the world. She got up and walked over to the window again to look at the road below, and the river across that road which flowed for miles through the pretty limestone valley.

'Pretty as a picture,' she whispered against Tiff's ear, and the baby blinked at her and yawned.

The promenade alongside the river opposite her flat was deserted, and traffic was light as it was still quite early in the morning. Several cars were at the roadside though, and she watched as another came slowly through from the more northerly town of Buxton, its driver obviously looking for a space to park.

It was a big car. Dark blue, with an up-to-the-minute registration number. It found a spot, eased into it, reversed to make it level with the pavement, then stopped.

In her arms Tiffany snuffled and wriggled. Cass laughed down into her dark baby eyes. 'Are you hungry?' She turned away from the window to sit by a low table where

Tiff's bottle was being kept warm. She tested the temperature of the milk, then began to feed the baby.

Tiffany sucked hungrily on the teat, and Cass got up with her still in her arms and walked over to the window again.

The morning sun was high in the sky and for a moment its glare on the glass blinded her as she allowed her gaze to drift back to the scene beyond the window. For some reason she was drawn there again, wondering what the driver of that car was doing now.

The car was empty, but there was a man on the opposite side of the road who hadn't been there before. He was looking at the river, and as she watched, he lifted something up to his face and although his back was to her, she knew what he was doing. People took photographs all the time along this stretch of the river, it was so pretty with its overhanging trees and baby ducklings swimming in the water. At this time of year though – early springtime – Rydale Tor was almost deserted. The tourists would come later, when the rhododendrons opened up on the high terraces, and the cherry tree blossom confettied the pavements.

The man pocketed the small camera and swung away from the river, looking up and down the road as if wondering what to do next. He was right opposite her now, his head half averted as he watched a cyclist coming towards him. As the cyclist passed, his head turned to look for traffic from the opposite direction, and for the first time she saw his face fully.

Shock made her edge away from the window, and her breath came out in a gasp of dismay.

'Patric!'

He walked back across the road towards his parked car, and her mind was whirling. He couldn't see her, of course. She was standing at the window of her flat – over the top of an empty 'For Sale' shop. And she was hidden behind gauzy curtains, cradling her baby in her arms. She dared to lean forward towards the window again, staring, and not quite believing – yet she had to believe, because he was there, right down there below her, just the same as she'd always remembered him – and yet – different somehow.

His hair – it was styled in a more up to date manner. It was close-cropped now and a lot more modern than the old Patric had ever worn it. His face seemed thinner too, lending him a lean, almost angry look. He was wearing brown – a light brown high necked sweater beneath a brown leather jacket. In the past he had always dressed conservatively, his usual attire being a dark, navy blue suit for business at boardroom level, and well-cut jeans and sweater when he was where he loved to be – down in the pit garages of the race track... Could this changed man really be Patric?

If it was, she decided she liked the new Patric, and she watched him keenly, having to forcibly fight back the desire to rap on the window and call out to him. How would she feel, she wondered, if she saw him rushing towards her, eager to catch her in his arms, and smother her with kisses. She closed her eyes briefly, her imagination moulding his body to hers, stirring up all kinds of memories, and aching so much for his touch.

'Idiot! It's probably not him at all.' Her eyes flew open and she pressed her face up close against the gauze curtains again and watched him as he loped off towards his car – the big dark blue one. But even half believing and half disbelieving it was him, she heard herself whispering urgently, 'Don't go, Patric...don't go...' But he drove away and her voice petered out on a sigh.

But why was he here, she wondered uneasily? For what reason had he parked the car and taken that photograph?

Had he somehow found out where she was?

No. That couldn't be it. He'd never even looked at the flat with the empty shop underneath it.

Tiffany was getting restless in her arms. Trembling, she moved away from the window, placing the feeding bottle on the coffee table before sitting down on the couch to burp the baby. Normality returned. A baby did that for you. She smiled. They took up so much of your time, there was little time for brooding. And anyway, she could have been mistaken, she supposed. Now that the car and the man had gone, she could almost convince herself that it hadn't been Patric…

The phone rang, and with Tiffany tucked up against her chest, Cass went to answer it. It was a familiar voice.

'Greer! Hi!' Tiffany gurgled and burped again, and Cass laughed.

'Cass – did you want me to come over today? It's not like me to be so addle-headed but I was out in Derby clubbing last night, and for the life of me I couldn't remember when I woke up ten minutes ago, whether or not you'd said you wanted me to have Tiff today.'

'No, love. It's Saturday – remember? I shall pop her in her buggy and take a walk to the shops, so make the most of your weekend – I'm going to be really tied up with this filming soon so you'll have your hands full with my darling daughter then.'

The girl on the other end of the line said, 'I'd like to come over though – if you don't mind. I want Tiff to get to know me so she doesn't miss you so much when you're working.'

'That's great then,' Cass replied. 'I'll wait for you – and we can do the shops together.'

'I'll be there in ten minutes.' There was a smile in the voice now. Greer was seldom without a smile. She was quite the most easy going – and dependable – teenager that Cass had ever known. And fresh out of college with all the necessary nursery-nurse certificates, Cass considered she'd been lucky to get her as a minder for Tiff.

After she'd put the phone down, Cass began getting Tiffany ready for the shopping trip, slipping the baby into her teddy-fleece-suit, fastening her into her buggy, and humming as she did so. It would be nice to have Greer for company, she decided. Babies were all very well, and she loved Tiff to bits, but babies weren't tops for conversation – not five month old ones anyway.

Greer arrived as she'd said she would – within ten minutes of the phone call, and they set off together down the main street of Rydale, stopping off first of all at the newsagent's kiosk on the riverside for Cass's Saturday newspaper and her usual monthly baby magazine. Greer had taken charge of Tiffany and the buggy and was now sitting on a bench overlooking the river where the baby could see the ducks dipping and diving in the water a few yards away. Tiffany loved watching the ducks, and Cass had taken to bringing a few slices of bread across the road to feed them sometimes. Tiffany would squeal and bang her hands up and down on the front apron of her buggy when they came out of the water, and strutted about, fighting for crumbs right up near to her.

Cass watched Greer with the baby from her place in the queue of three or four people buying newspapers and chocolate, but Tiffany, even at this young age was an independent little cuss, and she wasn't worried about Mummy, she was too interested in the ducks. She sat cooing and waving her arms at them, making an elderly couple on another bench nearby chuckle with laughter at her antics. Cass stood waiting to be served, and then turned back towards Greer's bench but came up against something brown and solid as she did so.

'I thought it was you. And then I thought it couldn't possibly be…'

Familiar dark eyes, and a new hairstyle, seen now at close quarters – made him devastatingly attractive. A hard hand gripping her arm made her startlingly aware of the fact that this was indeed Patric – and in the flesh this time, not seen merely through a first floor window.

He blinked. Half-reached out his other hand towards her too, not quite touching her cheek. Then she saw him swallow, and heard him say again hoarsely, 'Cass? Cass? Is it…' in a distant and faltering way, as if he couldn't quite believe his eyes.

She forced herself to stay calm. It was the most difficult thing she'd ever done in her life to smile, and say, just as if he were any old acquaintance she'd just come across, 'Patric!' Her smile was pure play-acting – glued on with sheer fright and the overwhelming need to appear perfectly normal. 'What a surprise!'

chapter two

All she heard was the one word being repeated and repeated though – in every question he asked. 'Why?'

'*Why* did you go off like that? *Why* didn't you tell me where you were going? *Why* the hell couldn't you trust me, Cass?' He sounded bitter and condemning.

'You know why,' she cried. 'Michelle needed you. I couldn't stand between you and her, not after what happened and she turned to you for help.'

'She killed a man with her dangerous driving,' he said. 'Did you really think I could forgive that? Cass – you know damn well that there was nothing left of our marriage; it was over and done with – years ago. She'd been having an affair with Craig Andrews for months, and we were already divorced when she had that accident.'

'But she came back to live with you.'

He sighed. 'There was no one else she could turn to. Yes – I know that, Cass. I told you the reasons for her returning home and you agreed it was the right thing. But there was never anything between us, it wasn't a permanent arrangement. Do you think I would have let myself fall in love with *you* if I'd still had any feelings for her? Years before you and I realised we had something special going for us, things had turned sour betwcen Michelle and me.'

Slowly she shook her head as she feasted her eyes on his face. She'd forgotten what it could be like, standing this close to him, feeling his hands on her, seeing his face – his dear, darling face, in front of her. 'But I thought…and Michelle said…'

He looked at her puzzled. 'Michelle said? What did Michelle say? I didn't know you and Michelle had ever spoken.'

Cass wished the words hadn't just tumbled out like that. She knew she had to explain however. 'She called me on the phone, while I was still in Suffolk – just after she'd come out of hospital. She said you two were getting along better – 'like the old days' were her exact words…she gave broad hints that the divorce had been a mistake and you both had a better understanding of each other…Patric – she actually told me you were both of a mind to get married again…'

Patric closed his eyes and said in a seething voice, 'Oh, no. No, Cass. Why didn't you tell me about that phone call?'

Michelle said it was best if I just made myself scarce. She said you were lovers again – and I just couldn't face you after that.'

'Oh, no!' He gazed at her now and she saw genuine pain in his eyes. 'Cass – you *knew* I loved you. You must have known I could never love Michelle again.'

'I was confused.' She couldn't meet his eyes now, for aside from confusion had been the knowledge that she was pregnant with Tiffany all those months ago. And if Patric and Michelle were really trying to make a new start together, that knowledge alone would have only added an unnecessary burden.

'But what are you doing here?'

His voice cut into her thoughts. Her mind began to work rapidly as she kept a sharp eye on Tiffany who was still entranced by the ducks on the river. 'Just…passing through,' she lied, knowing she had to keep him at bay until she knew if Michelle was still on his particular scene or not.

'Another assignment for a magazine – a photographic session?'

'Yes,' she said. 'You know me – I'm the originator of the word *workaholic*.'

'Where are you heading?'

'Manchester.' She said the first place name that came into her head, not feeling the slightest twinge of conscience at the second lie. She couldn't let him know the truth – that she actually lived here – *and* was bringing his daughter up in a flat not fifty yards away from where they were standing. Nor could she let him know that the same daughter, his baby, *her* Tiffany, was sitting in her buggy two strides away, laughing at the ducks with her childminder.

'What are you doing here? Buying newspapers?'

Guiltily, her free hand tightened on the newspaper and baby magazine which she'd folded inside it. 'Just buying a paper – and asking if they had a street map…of Manchester.' Another lie. It was right what they said. Once you started, there was no stopping. 'I don't know Manchester all that well.'

'You expected to find a street map of Manchester? This far away? In a riverside news kiosk of a sleepy little Derbyshire town?'

'I guess I made a mistake – going to the kiosk. It was just a spur of the moment thing, I didn't realise they wouldn't sell street maps. I guess I'll have to try and find a proper bookshop.'

'Where's your car?' he asked, his voice suddenly suspicious, and his hand fell away from her arm.

'Oh,' she waved a hand airily in the direction of a little twisting street that led up a hill across the road from them.

'Up there.' This was the truth. She always kept her car round the back of the houses and off the main thoroughfare. The next bit was pure invention however, 'I thought if I could get to the top of that hill, I might be able to take one or two good shots of that giant lump of limestone they call the 'Tor' around here. County magazines are always looking for new slants on well-known objects and places of interest.'

'When do you have to be in Manchester?'

'Oh, not for ages.' Not ever – her mind screamed – but she dare not tell him that.

'The woman – in the kiosk. She seemed to know you.' There was another hint of suspicion in his voice. 'You seemed on very friendly terms as she handed you your change.'

She laughed. 'They're friendly people up here in Derbyshire. They treat everybody like they're their next door neighbour.'

He stared across the road at the street she'd indicated which was right next to her flat and the dusty bare shop window underneath it. 'I don't see any car.'

She prayed he wouldn't start asking awkward questions, but so far there was nothing to connect her with the empty shop with the 'For Sale' notice in its window. She wondered what he'd think if he knew the truth however, that she'd already put in an offer for the place, and intended turning the bare showroom into a photographic studio very soon now. Tiffany had been taking up all her spare time of late or else her name might have been blazoned over the shop window and doorway by now.

Tiffany! She closed her eyes momentarily and looked past him at the baby again. But Tiff was lying back in the buggy now, her eyelids drooping, and Greer was pushing the buggy back and forward in a soothing motion. Cass knew the signs. Tiff was dropping off to sleep.

'I'm not going to let you go now that I've found you.' His voice was harsh and the expression on his face very stubborn.

Steadily, she looked at him. 'I've told you – I'm on my way to a job – in Manchester. I can't hang around here for long.'

'Give me an address then. A phone number. Somewhere I can reach you again, for heaven's sake.' He was becoming irate.

Her mind worked swiftly. 'I don't have a permanent address. I've been in a series of bed and breakfasts since I sold Mum's house in Suffolk.'

'Where?' he snapped. 'Where the hell have you been?'

'Derby.' She shrugged. 'Mainly Derby.' It was half a truth. After leaving Suffolk she'd spent a couple of weeks in the city – mainly doing the rounds of estate agents and driving round the countryside looking for somewhere to live.

'So when are you going back there? To Derby.'

'I'm *not* going back. I'm…er…going to stay with a friend.'

'In Manchester?' He raised one dark brow, obviously not believing a word she was saying. 'You expect me to believe that? You've never mentioned a friend in Manchester to me before.'

She'd done a little play-acting at school. Years ago. She'd also, quite recently, finished writing a screenplay for Aaron Trent, an American film director. Trent was an egocentric charmer who had to have his own way. He absolutely refused to call her Cass – saying the name Cassandra was old-fashioned and insisting on calling her 'Sandie' instead

– 'much more approachable baby – more of this world – and not some Victorian school-marm's name.'

She recalled Trent ranting and raving over the phone at her at one point during her work on the script. 'This won't do, Sandie-baby! We've gotta make this character thoroughly believable! She needs to be more convincing. Dammit – make her mad, make her bad if you like, but for God's sake – make her less wooden.'

She'd been so angry at him for his outburst that she'd put all her pent up fury into the character. She rounded on Patric Faulkner now, and using the exact words her character had used in the screenplay, she railed at him. 'Don't you dare treat me like this – as if I'm some trivial little *belonging* you'd lost and just found again, and now all you want to do is lock me up safely in your trophy cupboard.'

There, at that point, the particular scene had ended but it had helped her to get started – where Patric was concerned at least – and it was easy now to finish with, 'And don't you dare try to come back into my life,' she blazed. 'I don't have to answer to you for my actions, Patric. I've told you – I'm here to do a job and if you don't believe that, well tough!' She made a fist and thumped her chest. 'I'm my own person, Patric.' She lowered her voice to inject a new meaning into her words. 'I have a life of my own, and if you can't cope with that – well it would have been better if we'd never met up again.'

He stepped back from her, head high, eyes furious. After several tension-packed moments he said, 'You've changed. You've changed a hell of a lot, Cass. And I don't know if I like the new you.'

'Yes,' she said, 'I've changed and I'm glad of it. You don't know me at all now, Patric. I'm a different person to the one you knew in our sleepy old Suffolk village.'

Slowly he shook his head as he looked her up and down. 'Even your clothes – that multi-coloured top thing – you never wore vibrant colours like that before.'

'I do now.' She might have added that it was for Tiffany that she wore bright colours. The baby loved them. Her little face would light up and her hands reach out towards bright colours.

'Your hair too – you've let it grow. That's why I didn't recognise you at first – why I thought I must be mistaken…'

Tiffany was to blame for her hair too. She didn't have time for weekly visits to the hairdresser now – and it was all part and parcel of Cass's new relaxed lifestyle. Bright colours, long hair, coupled with a fierce determination to rely on herself for what she wanted out of life and not have to depend on anyone else – and especially not a man – not Patric!

Twelve months ago, change had been a necessary evil – but now she was glad of that change and she blessed the fates that had brought her here to Derbyshire. Daily, almost, she found herself thanking providence for the people who had played a part in bringing her here – first of all Roberta, her editor on the magazine in London where she'd worked – Roberta who, a couple of years ago, had sent her to photograph and report on a local, struggling group of actors who were fighting a demolition order of their much-loved little theatre in the east end of London. There, due to her initial publicity shots, she'd met American TV director, Aaron Trent, who had also taken up arms to help the group. He was in England making a documentary about the actors trying to save the theatre.

She and Trent had got along well together and he'd told her about plans he had to do some 'county' work he was interested in to take back to the states. Her mind flew back now to the days she'd worked tirelessly alongside Trent…

'Do me a screenplay, huh, honey? I might make a name for you if you can come up with a catchy theme.'

'I wouldn't know how to start.' She'd laughed.

'You're a photographer, dammit. All that 'visual' stuff should appeal to you. My next project's in a place called the Peak District. Derbyshire. Doesn't that appeal to you? All them there dark brooding mountains and moors? There's this village there where the plague was dumped on them from a parcel of clothing sent from London.' Aaron Trent had an infectious grin. He gave her a challenge. 'You've got six months before that, Sandie, so go to it, baby. Do me a script about the plague village – present day though – about star-crossed lovers or some such thing, huh – and I might make a name for you in TV?'

And now the reality was almost upon her and, while she knew without a doubt that she still loved Patric Faulkner, she certainly had no wish to go back to that half-life with him – a life where Michelle, his one-time wife, still held sway with him. No! That was finished. There was no future in that particular relationship any more and she had to convince him of that.

'You look absolutely stunning in bright colours – and with long hair,' he said softly and she began to weaken. Harsh words she could deal with, but this…this was different, hearing his voice – that tone, the way he used to talk to her…seeing his smile – the smile she could always bring to his lips…remembering so much about him that had made her happy…remembering his love-making…

'Don't come that,' she said, making her voice hard. 'You know I don't fall for flattery of any sort.'

'I mean it. It's not flattery.' He took a step towards her, clenched his hands into tight balls of exasperation as he appealed to her. 'Cass – you know me better than that. I say what I mean – and I mean it when I tell you now that you are more beautiful than ever – and I still feel the same way I did about you a year ago.'

She was weakening again. She felt flustered. She glanced at Tiffany again. The baby was sound asleep, and Greer avoided her gaze, obviously trying to keep well clear of the altercation between her employer and this strange man.

Cass looked back at him. 'I know you mean what you say, Patric, and I'm sorry, but things are different for me now.' She dared say no more. She just stood looking at him.

'Cass…' He reached out to her and pulled her into his arms.

'No!' She made herself rigid. 'No. This is wrong…'

His mouth drowned her objections and almost without conscious knowledge of what she was doing, she closed her eyes and began to respond to him. All around them was silence; there were no tourists, no shoppers, even on the riverside walk. The elderly couple were still sitting on the next bench to Greer and Tiff, but their eyes were half-closed, and it was a warm spring morning in a picturesque and drowsy little town. Her lips clung to his, her fingers dug into the soft leather of his coat against his shoulders. Thoughts were flying in and out of her mind. Damn Michelle! To hell with Michelle! Michelle didn't want him. Michelle didn't deserve him. Why shouldn't baby Tiff have a daddy…? And why should Patric be deprived of the knowledge that he had a child?

'No!' Suddenly she came to vibrant life and sprang away from him. It was no good thinking thoughts like that. Michelle was alive and Michelle needed him. He had a duty to look after her…and while Michelle was around, Cass knew she herself could have no real part of his life.

'Oh, God! No. No. We can't start all that up again.' She backed away from him.

He stood, unsure of himself if his expression was anything to go by, and she hated herself for what she'd just done. She should never have let him kiss her like that. It was wrong. While he was still sharing a house with Michelle, it seemed to her as if he was still married to the woman. It was all wrong.

He didn't speak. He just looked at her. She couldn't tell what he was thinking though, she just had to guess – and he looked so sad, so lost.

'Just go,' she said, her voice tense. 'Just get out of my life will you, Patric?'

He answered her. 'Not until you give me an address or a phone number. I need to be able to contact you again. I can't risk losing you now that I've seen you – found you – we need to talk, to communicate, Cass.'

'There's no point in that.' Inside, her heart was weeping. To the world, and to Patric however, she showed no emotion. Emotion was a killer; she made her face cold and hard to hide the hurt. Hurt she could do without. There'd been too much of that in her life in the past.

'We can work something out,' he said. 'Cass, believe me. I've already moved out of the house I lived in with Michelle. I pay people now to take care of her – a house-keeper, a nurse…'

Cass knew though that Michelle wouldn't give up easily. She'd hang on in there with Patric for as long as she could. And she didn't want happiness at any price – not at the price of him throwing a helpless, crippled woman out of his home and his life… What happiness could she and Patric enjoy knowing he'd been so heartless? 'You can't just turn your back on her now she's so helpless,' she said. 'It would be too cruel.'

'Cruel? To Michelle?'

'Of course – to Michelle.'

'But it's over, Cass. There's no marriage left.' He held out a hand, pleading with her to believe him. 'I've told you – we don't even live under the same roof any more.'

'You have a duty to her,' she said in a quiet, stony voice. 'And I couldn't be happy knowing I'm taking you away from a woman who was so badly injured that she deserves to be looked after.'

'I don't care a toss for duty. Michelle has no claim on me.'

She knew it was an explosion of all the misery he'd kept tightly controlled for so many months, but she could do nothing, say nothing to help him. She closed her lips tightly.

He went on, 'Damn duty and damn Michelle. And damn anything and everything that has made me lose you.' He was breathing heavily. He took a stride towards her. He stood in front of her. His eyes were tortured, his face a livid blur before her. 'I need you, Cass. I want you. Hell! I want you so much…'

She wanted to melt into his arms, but didn't dare do that. Briefly, she closed her eyes and then she remembered Tiffany, and she knew she just had to make him go – before Tiff woke up.

'Just go,' she seethed. 'Just get out of my life, damn you.'

'You said you were going to Manchester.' He was keeping a tight control on himself, she could see that.

'I am.' She tossed her head flippantly.

'If that's the case – if you're telling me the truth, then go. Now. Go to Manchester. Let me see you get into your car and drive away.'

Her head jerked up. 'So you can follow me?'

'No,' he said, gently now. 'I wouldn't do that. I wouldn't hound you. But I don't believe Manchester. I think you're living *here*. Somewhere near here anyway. But I just can't put my finger on why you'd be doing that.'

She tried to turn the attention away from herself. 'Why are *you* here?' she asked. 'If you aren't hounding me and following me, just tell me that.'

'A bit of business,' he said. 'Nothing you'd know about. Something that's not remotely connected with the motor-racing world I'm involved with – although the bloke who's hired me seems to think I'm the eyes and the ears of the world when it comes to race circuits.'

'You're branching out?' The words were glib, as if she didn't care. 'Good for you.'

'No. Nothing like that. Just repaying a favour.'

'Oh, yes?'

'Yes,' he said, and clamed up. He obviously wasn't going to enlighten her any further.

'And Michelle?'

'She's joining me. Later. She's down in Suffolk at the moment. Still at the house. She had to give up her job – sold the herb business she'd built up, but I expect you knew that. She's getting bored now though.'

She swallowed. He was staying in Derbyshire. She didn't think she could stand it, knowing he was so near. 'Where are you staying?' Her voice had turned husky. Please, she prayed, please don't let him be hanging out anywhere near Rydale Tor.

'Out on the moors above Buxton.'

She breathed easily again. It was a good distance away. 'For how long?'

He shook his head. 'Goodness knows. Just till the job is finished. Can I see you again?'

'I told you – I'll be in Manchester.'

'I could drive up there to see you. Manchester's not so very far.'

'No. That wouldn't be a good idea.'

'Give me a phone number – or an address.'

She was beginning to feel decidedly pressured, and she didn't like it. 'Hell – you sound like an old-fashioned gramophone that's got its needle stuck,' she burst out. 'Give me a break will you…?'

'I mean it, Cass – I'm not budging until I know where I can contact you again.'

She let out a long sigh. She knew he meant what he said, and if she turned awkward, she also knew that he'd never let up until he found her again, despite what he'd said about not hounding her.

Her mind worked swiftly. 'A phone number. I can give you a number. Will that satisfy you?'

Quietly he said, 'Yes. It's a start.'

'I don't want any hassle though,' she warned.

'Have I ever…'

'No,' she cut in quickly. 'No – not until today.'

He reached inside his jacket and then held out a pen and organiser to her.

'Write it down.'

She took the things from him, wrote down her mobile phone number and handed the organiser and pen back to him. There was no way he'd be able to trace her from a mobile phone number.

He looked at what she'd written. 'This isn't a Manchester code. This is a mobile…'

'Yes,' she said. 'It is. I'm often out and about, and I don't see the necessity for a permanent line yet – not until I find somewhere I want to settle.'

His eyes narrowed. 'I have this feeling that what you said about Manchester isn't entirely true.'

'I have a reason.' She faced him, never flinching.

'Somebody else? Is there somebody else in your life? And you don't want things messing up?'

There was Tiff. She wasn't lying any more when she said, 'Yes. There's somebody else. You being on the scene could make things awkward – could complicate matters in a big way.'

'You love him?' He was direct and to the point, and very, very cold towards her now. 'Is it serious? Will it last?'

'Yes,' she said. 'It's serious. It *will* last. Forever. It's that kind of relationship. It's nothing like the relationship you and I shared, Patric. It's a completely different feeling I have for this other person.'

'I see.' His voice was hard, his eyes cold.

She wanted to rush into his arms, wanted to explain that there *wasn't* anyone else – not a man anyway. There was just Tiffany who she loved with all her heart and mind and soul, and she was telling no lies this time when she'd said the relationship was one that would last forever.

But she couldn't tell him the absolute truth. Knowing about Tiff would bind him to her more tightly than anything else in the word could bind him. And she didn't want that. Not when he was already bound to Michelle, his wife, who needed him and had first claim on him.

Michelle was the one who mattered, and Cass knew she couldn't deliberately prise him away from the woman who had nothing else to live for but *him*. She had to let him go.

'Do you still want to keep that phone number?' she asked.

He looked down at the neat, black organiser in his hand. 'Yes,' he said. 'I think I do.'

She watched him walk away from her and out of her life again and, surprisingly, when he got into his car he never spared her a backward glance.

And when he'd driven away and was safely out of sight, she took the buggy and she and Greer carried on down the High Street to do her weekend shopping as if nothing had happened.

But inside, in her heart, it was a different matter. And that heart, just at the moment, was feeling more than a little bit bruised and battered. It would have been so easy in some ways, to start up the relationship again – so hard in others though, knowing that Patric would have no peace of mind if he had to choose between two people who both had a claim to him – first his wife, and then, of course, little Tiffany – the daughter he didn't even know about.

She caught Greer glancing at her in a funny sort of way a time or two during the next few minutes, and she realised that the girl must have seen something of the encounter between her and Patric. Greer had a right to know anyway, she decided, so she suggested dropping in at a small café in the high street, and there she told the girl about Patric – and about Tiffany too, in the simplest way possible.

Greer needed to know, after all, that Patric must be kept in the dark about Tiffany at all costs. Cass couldn't risk him coming back into her life again just as things were working out for her.

chapter three

It was a typical weekend homecoming, Patric Faulkner thought grimly, and one he was rapidly growing accustomed to nowadays.

If he only missed seeing her for a day, Michelle would start making all sorts of accusations, so after a whole weekend away in Derbyshire, he was amazed that she hadn't begun on him as soon as he walked through the front door but had actually allowed him to get into the drawing room before the tirade began.

'Are you still seeing her behind my back?' Her voice rose to a shrill scream. 'You're still in love with that damn Fairburn girl, aren't you? You're besotted – utterly besotted with her.' The words turned ugly. 'Are you still carrying on an affair with her? Are you still seeing her?'

She stood in front of the ornate marble fireplace, supporting her fragile weight on two arm-crutches. She wore a black cashmere sweater and long black skirt that reached her ankles. Black was her colour these days. She'd never worn any other shade since Craig's death – and her own near tragic accident.

Patric swung round from the wide window of the house he'd shared with her until recently, since the day they'd married more than ten years ago. It overlooked the sea and was situated in the small Suffolk village he'd been brought up in. Since the divorce though, he'd moved out and now had a small sea-front flat half-a-mile away. He still saw Michelle regularly though. Divorced they might be, but she was the clinging sort and his phone never stopped ringing if he didn't pop in at least once a day to see how she was.

His voice was raw with pain as he replied to his one-time wife, 'Of course I'm not having an affair – with Cass or anyone. How the hell do you expect me to find the time for anything like that when you're always making demands, always watching, always questioning…'

'You've been up there in Derbyshire for two whole days, dammit.' Her eyes blazed into his. 'I couldn't keep tabs on you while you were there, could I? And I only have your word for it that you've been *working*.'

'I *have* been working.' Patric swung round to watch the sea again. Watching anything at all was better than facing her rage and her tantrums. He didn't see why he should have to explain himself though. He had nothing to feel guilty about, he told himself.

'Work! Hah! You call it work? Watching a bunch of lunatic motor-cyclists race around country lanes, trying to break their damned necks?'

'You're the expert in the field of speeding round country lanes.' The words – softly spoken – were out before he had time to bite them back, and they hit home.

She screamed at him again. 'Oh, don't let me forget it, will you? Don't *ever* let me forget that because of my speed in the car that night, I ended up with my legs smashed to pieces – and my baby dead.'

'I wasn't thinking just of you.' He turned to face her again. He'd got her off the subject of Cass for the moment and he wasn't sorry for what he'd said about the accident.

It was time for it to be said, he decided. She was no longer the helpless invalid she'd been in hospital for all those months. He looked at her, reflecting that she was still a beautiful woman, a striking one too, with that dark olive complexion that had no flaw in it. She could still command attention; she'd have no trouble getting a man if that's what she wanted – even though for a lot of the time she used a wheelchair to get around in.

She wasn't helpless though – far from it. She was powerful in her own right, and she could walk a little now – with the crutches. In the past she'd been super-woman however. She'd had her own business, her own little empire, her own money, and he knew how she missed 'being in charge'.

At the moment, she wasn't at her best. Her face was twisted with rage and impotent fury. Rage wasn't always an outward thing with her, more often than not it was something that came from deep within her, a desperate kind of devil that drove her – like the time when he had first suggested moving out after she'd been home from hospital several months, and she'd thrown herself down the stairs in a tantrum – just to keep him there. When she was in a mood like that there was no helping her, no reasoning with her. When she got a bee in her bonnet about something – as she had at the moment – somebody was going to suffer. And all too often, Patric knew he was the one who bore the brunt of her volatile temper.

'You hate me, don't you?' Her eyes were cruelly calculating, but in her voice was a demand for contradiction. She didn't want him to hate her. She wanted to be loved, adored, admired, he knew. He couldn't give her any of those things though, and living with her, being forced to remember her treachery day after day, was not a recipe for reconciliation. Living with her had just not worked out.

'Yes,' he said, not attempting to disguise the fact any longer. 'You know I do. I think I'd hate anybody who could kill in cold blood – and then never shed a compassionate tear nor wrestle with their conscience afterwards. I abhor what you did. I despise you for hiding behind your own accident and escaping blame for what was, in fact, an act of murder.'

More calmly now she faced him, her chin jutting aggressively in a way he knew well as she replied, 'I hate you too. I hate your bloody guts. So that makes us equal.'

He lifted his shoulders in a shrug. 'Tell me something I don't know,' he said, 'I know perfectly well that you hate me. We've nothing in common any more, Michelle. Haven't had since way before the accident. Why else would you have taken up with Craig Andrews – a man young enough to…'

'Don't say it. Don't dare say he was young enough to be my son, because he wasn't,' she snapped. 'Craig wasn't all that much younger than I was.'

He walked towards her. 'I was going to say he was young enough – and good looking enough – to have any woman he wanted.'

'Liar,' she blazed.

'It's true though isn't it? So why don't you want to talk about Craig Andrews? At one time you never stopped talking about him, and comparing us – to my obvious detriment. You never stopped telling me that *he* knew how to treat a woman properly; constantly singing *his* praises at every opportunity. Come on, Michelle, why can't we talk about him now?'

She glanced at him, then away again. 'Craig's dead, and he deserved everything that happened to him.'

'Doesn't it worry you that you murdered him?' Patric said.

Her head swivelled back to him. 'I was never found guilty of murder.'

'You were never put on trial, you were too badly injured,'

he pointed out. 'But *you* know, and *I* know, it was no accident, Michelle. It was murder in every sense of the word.'

'I paid for it.' Her voice was rising again. 'Look at me. A bloody cripple – tied for the rest of my life to that wheelchair.' She jerked her head towards the chair in question, tucked neatly away in a corner of the room.

Coldly he said, 'Don't ask me for pity, Michelle – at least you *do have* the rest of your life – unlike poor Craig Andrews. I didn't like the man, but I can't ever forget what you did to another human being – and one you professed to love. And you're not tied to a wheelchair,' he went on dispassionately. 'You can get around fine now without the chair if you put your mind to it.'

'I don't call this 'fine'! She looked down at her long skirt, and then stabbed a glare at him to say, 'I didn't crash the damned car on purpose…'

'…*After* you killed Craig,' he broke in. 'Why don't you finish the sentence and admit that you killed him deliberately then drove away in such a rage that you didn't know what you were doing.'

'It was never proven. My foot could have slipped on the accelerator and made me drive into Craig.' She was haughty and cool again.

'And then you just happened to drive off and leave him there – dying in the driveway of 'Lilacs', your old family home, the place that – unbeknown to me – had been your love nest,' he pointed out grimly.

'I was in shock when I drove away. I didn't know what I was doing.' Her voice was shaking now. 'In the hospital, after the accident, I had counselling – therapy – and it all became clear to me – I was devastated because I'd *accidentally* killed Craig. It was panic, pure panic that made me drive away…'

He couldn't feel sorry for her – couldn't feel anything except cold hatred. 'So you crashed the car – in panic.'

'That was how it happened. I – I wasn't thinking straight.'

'Yes,' he said. 'I've heard it all so often, I sometimes find myself starting to believe it too. I never actually come to the point of believing it whole-heartedly though – not like you do.'

'I hate you.' Her temper flared again, almost to the point of hysteria.

'Yes,' he said. 'I heard you the first time.'

'But I'll never let you go. You know that, don't you?'

'Yes,' he said in a dull voice. 'I know you of old, Michelle. You've lost your toy-boy, so now anybody else will do – just as long as you have an audience. But this audience…' Raising a clenched fist he banged it hard on his chest. '…*This* particular audience isn't going to be fooled into thinking you need pity.'

'You were my husband once. Not even you would walk out on me – not now that I'm so utterly dependent on you.'

'I have walked out,' he said. 'I have the flat now, but if I ever walk out on you for good, you've got plenty of people who'll make life easy for you. You've got the housekeeper and the nurse – people who are paid to look after you. I make damn sure you're OK, yet still I'm lumbered with you. You still treat me as if I'm married to you, Michelle – and I've had enough. There are going to be some changes in the future. This sort of half-life isn't working. We need to start behaving like reasonable, civilised people…and not always as a couple who are at loggerheads with each other.'

He could see his words had hit home. In all honesty, neither of them could dispute the fact that there was nothing left of what they'd once had. She forced an enthusiasm to her voice, however, for he'd promised her last week that he'd take her up to Derbyshire for a short break. She'd wheedled the promise out of him after telling him her doctor was treating her for depression…

'You've arranged the trip, though? To Derbyshire? For me? While you were up there? What's it like? I'm longing to see the place where you'll be working.'

'I took some photographs to show you. I dropped the film in at the shop so I'll collect them tomorrow.' He turned away from her.

'And we're really going there – together? At the end of the month?' she asked.

'Yes.'

He stood and flicked a remote control at the television set. The evening news programme was being broadcast. He didn't want to talk any more. Talking always ended up as arguing.

She snapped, 'Turn that off. I want to talk to you.'

'Michelle – I've driven a long way today. I want to relax. I just want to get back to the flat…'

'And be alone?' She shuffled across the floor to face him where he was standing. 'Do they know about *me* in Derbyshire?' she wanted to know. 'The film crew? And that director fellow from America – Aaron Trent?'

'I've told Aaron that my ex-wife is coming with me. He also knows that I've rented a bungalow on the moors above the town of Buxton for you.'

'Not just for me, darling. That will be nice. Just like old times.' Then she gave a mock shudder. 'A bungalow though? Won't that be minuscule? And what about the wheelchair?'

He switched off the television. 'Look,' he said, 'it's OK. It's a nice place. Not as big as here, I must admit, but I shall stay in a nearby hotel. I've arranged for somebody to come and cook and clean every day, and we'll be taking the nurse with us…'

'I don't want the damned nurse. I'll have you. You don't *have* to stay in a dreary hotel. And we're not taking Judy with us. I've given her a week or two off anyway.'

'I won't be there all the time to lavish you with attention,' he said sharply.

'But I refuse to be treated like a baby…'

'Stop acting like one then,' he said. 'It makes sense for Judy to come. OK?'

'No, it's not OK.' Her hands clenched tightly around the crutches. 'I refuse to be left out of things. If Judy's there, you'll go off and leave me to my own devices. And I want to meet Aaron Trent. He's getting to be quite a name. I refuse to be pushed into the background like a nobody…'

'You *will* meet him. But it's no place for a woman in your situation,' he pointed out. 'Filming starts in two weeks and there'll be motorbikes whizzing round every corner of the village. There'll be actors, the press, camera crews, lighting engineers, extras, sight-seers, the woman who wrote the damn screenplay et cetera, et cetera…'

'A woman.' Her head shot up. 'Oh, I see. There's a woman involved is there? So, *that's* why you want me out of the way! That's why you've tried to persuade me not to come with you to Derbyshire next time.'

'I'm going to do a job, Michelle. Aaron Trent wanted someone on the set with experience of racing bikes, and I have some experience of that, though not as much as I have of racing cars. I owe him a favour. Trent was one of the major sponsors for the Cambridge circuit; he put in a great deal of money for that little set up, you know that. I couldn't refuse when he asked me to help him out.'

'But the woman,' she insisted. 'Tell me about the woman.'

'I don't know *who* the damn woman is.' He was fast becoming exasperated. 'I haven't met her, and I see no reason why I should. She and Trent got together over the screenplay. He seems quite smitten with her work though. Talks about her as if she's got a bright future ahead of her.'

'Her name,' she snapped. 'What's her name.'

He stood up, walked to the window again, then turned round to face her. 'I think it's Sandra. I haven't met her myself, but Trent calls her Sandie.'

chapter four

'Why can't we clean that white stuff off the window?'

The blond spiky-haired young man, standing on steps and fixing what would, in time, be spot-lighting – in the shop below Cass's flat – yelled across the large room to her.

Cass winced at the noise, but carried on undercoating the skirting board with primer paint. 'Dillon Teasdale – do you have to raise your voice like that? I told you when I came down that Tiff had just gone off to sleep upstairs – and I don't want her waking just yet. I want to get the whole of this skirting finished today.'

'Heck! Sorry!' He grinned down at her and she couldn't be angry with him. He'd been such a great help to her, re-wiring the place at a ridiculously low price, as well as doing loads of the little mundane jobs around the place since she'd been here.

She rolled off her knees and sat looking up at him, her back leaning against a bit of wall where the skirting board hadn't yet been painted. 'Why do you want the whitewash stuff off the windows?'

'It hides the view outside. No ulterior motive. I just like the view from here, don't you?'

Cass shook her head and laughed up at him. 'It couldn't be anything to do with the fact that you like watching the girls walk past – giving you a chance to ogle them and drool over them?'

'Not a chance, darlin'! It's the girls that ogle me – not the other way round. Especially when I'm on the bike –

wearing me leathers.' He poked around with a screwdriver, pulled out a piece of wire from the ceiling and yelped, 'There! Got the bast – Oops – sorry Cass. I know you don't like me using that sort of language. But honestly, baby Tiff won't understand swear words for ages yet. And she *is* asleep upstairs.'

'I don't want to clean the window – not till the studio is all ready for folks outside to see I mean business. If they catch a glimpse of me like this – in paint-spattered overalls and my hair tied up in a scarf, they're hardly going to believe I can take gorgeous pictures of their kids and dogs, are they?'

But there was another reason why she didn't want people staring in – and that reason was Patric. If he'd found her once, he could do so again, though to her knowledge there had been no sign of him in Rydale Tor since that day a week ago.

Dillon Teasdale perched himself more comfortably on top of the wooden steps and rubbed at his chin with one hand. 'Some of 'em, the girls who make eyes at me in me bike leathers, they like stubble. What do you think, Cass? D'you think it's more macho? Would you fancy somebody who hadn't shaved for a week?'

'What do I think about stubble? Now there's a question!' She tried not to laugh. 'It's OK – on the right person, I suppose. You see a lot of film stars sporting stubble these days.'

'That Trent fellow who's making your film said to leave it – he wants at least five days growth of it when they start the cameras rolling.'

'Not much of your face will be showing surely – with a bike helmet covering your head.'

He shrugged. 'Trent said I might get a screen test –

without the lid on. Asked me a lot of questions about myself though – including, did I do drugs!'

Cass pulled a face. 'Is that a *for* or an *against* – when it comes to screen tests?'

'A definite *against*. He said he didn't want no trouble. Smoking ciggies was OK, swearing was OK, and even drinking in moderation, so long as I didn't spend all me time in the pub getting blotto.'

'So you told him…'

'I told him that a forty-hours-a-week electrician doesn't make the kind of money I'd need for drugs. All I earn is spent on the flippin' bike. Well, *you* know that, don't you? I get my kicks from the old ZX. It's all I ever wanted to do – ride! There's nothing like it. Power! Speed – and I'm serious, Cass – I mean the wheels kind of speed, not the other sort.'

'You must be a one-off. From what I read in the newspapers, it seems all youngsters try the other sort at some time or other.'

'Nah! It's vastly over-rated, believe me. The only time I did try it I was sick as a dog for days after – and that headache! Wow, did I have a daddy of a headache. And anyway – don't class me as a youngster, if you don't mind. I'm twenty-four,' he swaggered his broad shoulders a little and preened himself, flexing one brawny arm and looking approvingly at the muscle movement under the short sleeve of his black T-shirt. 'I'm just the right age for stardom – so sez Mister Trent. Can you see me in movies? The next diCaprio?' He punched the air and shouted, 'Yes!'

'With that amount of stubble – I can see you as the next "*Lassie*"!'

He aimed a clipped off bit of wire at her and she laughed and ducked so it missed her.

'Cheek! You'll respect me when I come back from the States a millionaire – but hey – what's that I hear outside?' He put one hand to his ear and assumed an expression of sheer ecstasy.

'At a guess, I'd say it's a motorbike,' Cass said sarcastically. 'Don't tell me you can't recognise the love of your life when you hear those far from dulcet tones coming down the road.'

He was down the wooden stepladder in a flash, quipping, 'Are you saying I prefer bikes to the real thing? If so – you're right, Cass. Bikes don't want you telling them all that mush about love – and you don't have to buy them chocs and flowers to make up after a row.'

'Which you'd never get diCaprio doing,' she said, making her voice wooden.

He stood still in the middle of the room listening to the powerful bike engine outside on the road, a look of pure bliss on his face. 'It's angelic,' he said in a mock whisper. 'Don't you agree? It's a Goldwing, of course. I'd recognise that fifteen twenty, six-cylinder little beauty anywhere. It beats drugs – and sex – hands down.'

She raised her eyes in mock despair and asked, 'Aren't you *ever* going to take a girl seriously? Honestly, Dillon, a bike won't cook a dinner for you – or do your washing.'

He grinned down at her again. 'Me Mam does those things well enough, Cass.'

'Lucky old you.' Cass leaned her head back on the cool wall and watched him as he sloped off across the bare wooden floorboards to rub an eye-hole in the whitewashed window so he could squint through it at the bike that had stopped outside one of the shops.

At last he turned to face her, laughing, his spiky blond hair sticking out at all angles, his good-looking face full of amusement. 'Girls,' he said, 'I've had 'em up to here.' He tapped the top of his head. 'All they want is a good time – and me muscled, perfect body of course…'

She scrambled to her feet and covered her ears with both hands. 'Oh, Dillon, stop it.' She was rocking with laughter now.

'Come on now.' He sprinted away from the window and pulled at her hands, dragging them away from her ears. He let them go, thrust his face forward and said, 'Go on – tell me that you're worried what young Tiff will say, if she hears me talking dirty. Will it be…'

She punched him in the midriff and he doubled up. 'I *know* what Tiff's first word will be,' she said, as he made a remarkable recovery and stood before her again.

'I bet you don't.'

'I bet I do.'

'What then? Go on – tell me? Which of my favourite four-letter words is it going to be?'

She shook her head, and still laughing she said, 'Not a four-letter one – unless I include 'bike' in the list.'

'Not a four-letter?' He rubbed thoughtfully at his chin.

'No.'

'Tell me then.'

'Kawasaki,' she said solemnly. 'Or maybe Goldwing – or Ducati – or Harley-Davidson.'

'Are you trying to tell me something?' He raised his fantastically dark-coloured brows that contrasted so starkly with his blond hair.

'That you have a one track mind about motorbikes? Yes!'

'I don't talk about them all that much, do I?'

She bent to pick up her paintbrush again. 'Not so you'd notice,' she tossed back over her shoulder. 'Only about ninety-five percent of the time anyway.'

'You mean I'm a bore?'

'A *very* nice bore.'

'Cass!'

'Look,' she turned on him. 'We've got work to do – and the sooner we do it, the sooner you're going to be able to get back to the bike.'

'Wish I'd got one like that outside though.' He shook his head. 'Heavy – but a real beauty that one. Goldwing. Yeah! It's heavy. It's like a Rolls-Royce, you know – the absolute cream of bikes. I've seen grown men lose it. It's like a baby elephant – but beautiful, man, really beautiful!'

'Watch it.' She grinned at him. 'You're turning green, I can see it from here.'

He sighed. 'Cass! I'm jealous as hell of anybody who owns such a bike.'

'Maybe Mister Trent will make your fortune for you.'

'Yeah, yeah. Pity I'm a realist, Cass. Money's never come easy to us Teasdales though.'

She was down on her knees again now, carefully stroking the laden brush along the skirting board. 'It never did to me either, Dill. I still can't believe that Aaron Trent had such faith in me writing that screenplay.'

He wagged his screw-driver at her as she glanced at him.

'It's even got a ruddy reverse gear, you know – that Gold-wing.'

'Wow!' she said, not impressed.

'You have no soul.' He sighed and climbed back up the step-ladder.

'When I see ten thousand other bikers and *you*, right outside my front door every weekend, and hear those bikes revving and waking Tiff up, I'm afraid I don't have a soul,' she said.

'You're exaggerating,' he said, 'Nobody could get ten

thousand motor bikes into Rydale Tor…'

'Hundreds then. They wake Tiff up when they come roaring into town – sometimes as early as seven o'clock on a Sunday morning.'

'It's a good place to meet. Good for trade as well – despite what some of the old fuddy-duddys of Rydale say.'

Cass laid her paintbrush across the top of the tin of paint and gazed up at him. 'They're harmless, I suppose, your biker friends. They just look a bit fierce in their leathers and helmets – and with those roaring monstrosities of motor-bikes underneath them.'

'You should come out and meet them one Sunday.'

'Oh, yes!' Her head jerked up. 'I can really imagine myself doing that – I don't think! What on earth would Tiff do if she was surrounded by all those beards and skull and cross-bones helmets?'

'She'd love it.' He grinned at her as he walked to the doorway and stood there holding on to the door post. 'Tiff is tougher than you think. One day, I'll whisk her off on the bike and I bet she'll love that too.'

'Over my dead body,' Cass said dryly.

'You're old-fashioned, Cass darlin'. You should start taking a few chances – you might find you enjoy it.' The laugh was lazy now.

'Haven't you ever been in love with a girl?' she asked, 'As opposed to a motorbike, I mean?'

'You're crazy, Cass. Bikes don't give you the hassle that women do. Give me a bike any day. Those lines, those curves, that purring pussy-cat engine. Wowee!'

She shrugged. 'OK! Be lonely then in your old age when your creaking joints stop you getting on a bike, and all you want is some nice woman to bring you a cup of tea as you sit in front of your lonely hearth…'

'Dreaming about bikes,' he murmured, gazing into space. Then he laughed and threw a duster at her. 'I'm not lonely. I'll never be bloody lonely.' He scrambled to his feet. 'I've got the gang for company. How can I be lonely? We'll all grow old together and sit in a corner of some pub, reminiscing about the good old days, and Harleys, and Ducatis, and…'

'Yeah, yeah! You *can* be lonely in a crowd though. Anyway, twenty or thirty bikers are hardly soul-mates, are they?'

'I never said I wanted a soul-mate.' He stood before her, his face flushing with embarrassment. 'Heck – that's the last thing I'd want – and forgive me for saying this Cass, but I think you're the *last* person on earth who should be giving me so-called 'auntie' advice. You've got little Tiff upstairs, but I see no obvious sign of a "soul-mate" on *your* horizon.'

The truth hit home. She realised he had a point. She grimaced and said, 'I asked for that, didn't I?'

'Sorry!' He looked suddenly shame-faced. 'I had no right to say it. It's your life, Cass.'

'Maybe not. But you hit the nail on the head. My life isn't exactly a bed of roses – and, no, there isn't a soul-mate around, but there was once.'

'Tiff's daddy?' He'd shoved his hands in his pockets now and was looking down on her from his six-feet two- inches of hunkiness.

She nodded, then decided it was best to avoid his gaze and get on with her painting. She gave all her attention to the next brushful of white gloss as she replied, 'Tell me I was young and naïve and I should have known better, if you want to.'

'Aw, Cass. I'm not the one to give advice.'

She gave a little laugh. 'I'm just kidding. I don't go shouting it around that I'm an unmarried mum.'

He hunched his shoulders. 'She's cute. Tiff. Does her daddy know about her?'

'No!' Her lips clamped shut. Already she'd said too much.

He was silent for some seconds, then said, 'If *I'd* fathered a kid, I'd want to know about it.'

'Why? So you could pay for its upkeep?' she asked sharply.

He blinked at her frankness. 'Well, no, but…'

'Just so you could boast about your virility to your mates?'

'Hell, Cass. No. It's natural though – to want a kid of your own.'

'Well just wait until you've got a bit of cash behind you,' Cass said. 'Make sure you're ready for responsibility, Dillon.'

'So you just upped and left him when you knew you were preggers with Tiff?' There was disbelief in his face as he stared at her.

She grinned at him. 'Something like that. But not quite so callous as you make it out to be.'

'What about Tiff?' The scowl was back again. Darker if anything.

'What about her?'

'What will you tell *her* about him?'

'I haven't decided yet. She's too young anyway.'

He shrugged. 'She'll be going to nursery school in another two years' time. She'll start asking questions. And the other kids will have mums *and* dads.'

'Oh, for heaven's sake, Dillon – what are you trying to do? Give me a conscience or something?'

'I used to ask questions about *my* dad,' he said. 'Mam would never talk about him though. I don't know to this day what he looked like, where he was from, or what his name was. There's a ruddy great gap in my life because I never had a dad.'

Cass put her paintbrush down across the top of the paint tin and slowly looked up at him. 'I'm sorry,' she said huskily. 'I never realised.'

He crouched down facing her. 'Cass – it's important,' he said. 'Don't ever lie to Tiffany. Tell her what it was like or, as she gets older, maybe she'll start to hate you...'

Conscience nagged at her enough without this. 'Don't look at me like that – like an abandoned spaniel pup,' she said.

'Tell her. Promise me you'll tell her.' He reached out, touched her face with an incredibly gentle gesture. 'Don't leave her in the dark like I was left – wondering and guessing, and not knowing if my Mam actually wanted me or not.'

'I never intended keeping her in the dark about her father.' She bit down on her lip.

'You loved him?'

She nodded. 'That's putting it mildly, Dill.' She gave a shaky sort of laugh.

'So why...'

'Don't ask!' she said.

'Maybe one day you'll get together with him again...'

'No!' She shook her head. 'No. That won't happen.'

'Poor Cass.' He stayed down on his haunches, watching her till she returned his stare, her eyes bright, but refusing to shed tears.

'I'm not *poor Cass*,' she said, her voice strong and without a waver.

'No. You were lucky,' he said. 'You landed on your feet – getting Aaron Trent interested in your work.'

'I realise that.' She gave a hard little laugh.

'You're made, Cass. There's talk on the set that he intends doing a follow-up to this intense one-off drama, maybe making a whole television series after filming's finished on this one.'

She nodded and said with a forced brightness, 'That's right. Aaron Trent's already asked me if I can come up with the goods. But even if I say no, I do have a profession I can fall back on.'

'Photography?' He gazed round the big room. 'This studio?'

'Mmm.' She nodded. 'That's why I bought the place.'

'I thought you hated the noise that the motorbikes make when they congregate outside here every weekend?'

She smiled. 'They bring the sight-seers into Rydale Tor,' she pointed out. 'You know that yourself. Rydale's a busy little place – even in winter we get the hardier breed of tourist to our "little English Switzerland".'

'And the film will get your name noticed,' he said thoughtfully. 'That's an added bonus, I suppose. Everybody will want their photographs taken by the new name in television drama. It'll be the next best thing to a "by Royal Appointment" won't it?' He grinned. 'I can see it now – plastered across the window – "*Aaron Trent approved*"!'

'You make it sound like I've been to bed with him. But seriously, Dillon, I haven't decided,' she said, 'whether to cash in on being "Sandie' Fairburn – screen-writer, or else be myself – "*Cassandra*" – photographer. I think that would be enough, don't you? Just "*Cassandra*" in black lettering with gold shading on the window? Time will tell, I suppose, which will suit me best.'

But, she thought silently to herself, the name 'Sandie' might give her a degree of anonymity – for the time being, at least.

She didn't dare risk Patric discovering he had a child – not until she'd got used to the idea herself.

chapter five

Aaron Trent, fiftyish, blond-haired and attractive, and with a torso any twenty-something would be proud of, under that brown suede shirt swinging open over a black T-shirt, came loping across Ashton-in-the Peak's marketplace towards Cass as she stepped out of her car.

'Sandie – sweetheart – where the hell can I get a truck-load of autumn leaves?' he wanted to know.

She was getting used to such questions, but still felt strange when she was addressed as *Sandie*. She finished locking up her car before turning to him and saying in as reasonable a tone as she could manage, 'Autumn leaves? At the end of May? Now there's a question.'

'We need them for the crash scene – the one where the bikers are racing through the village.' He held out a pair of huge hands to her. 'Sandie – think! Think hard. You wrote the damn story. I thought I could depend on you.' The hands dropped to his sides, smoothed themselves over the rough denim of his jeans. 'Hell – why do we keep running up against problems?'

She fell into step beside him as he strode out towards a barrage of lighting equipment and an assortment of vans and motor-homes on the other side of the square. 'We're going to have to leave that scene,' she said. 'There's no way I can think of anything that will magic up autumn leaves in springtime, and the film will be finished way before autumn.'

'Hell! Hell and damnation and fu…'

'Fuzz and furoré,' she broke in on his tirade, laughing. 'Don't say the four letter version,' she warned. 'I never wrote any four-letter words into that script – and you know I hate to hear that sort of language.'

He stopped short and grabbed hold of her shoulder, swinging her round to face him. He was laughing too now though, as he asked, 'What kinda guy do you think this is going to make me look like? Coming out with that stupid "fuzz and furoré" stuff in front of the damned crew?'

'My version of your four-letter word sounds a lot better than what you were going to say,' she replied, 'and the crew will know what you mean anyway.'

'Four-letter words have always gotten me what I wanted before, honey. They're words I've been using for the whole of my life. Do you hear me? The whole of my f…'

'Trent!' she broke in, 'I'm warning you.'

'Aw, Sandie-baby – don't patronise me.' The laughter had faded now. His strong jaw was set stubbornly. 'I don't need any dame trying to set me on the straight and narrow. What I need is leaves!'

She was being careful to watch where she was putting her feet as they walked because wires were trailing all over the place, and great arc lights had been set up, focusing on one gleaming, silver-and-black motorbike that was parked up near Ashton's stone war memorial with a couple of men bending down over it, examining its tyres.

There were onlookers by the score, kept back from the scene about to be filmed by barriers and men in security uniforms. They were causing no trouble – arriving every morning, clambering into their cars and mini-buses if the location changed, and following Aaron Trent's convoy of steep-sided trucks, jeeps, and trailers up winding Derbyshire roads and across steep grit-stone valleys. Their patience amazed Cass. All they wanted was to get a glimpse of what was happening in their tiny bit of England. They never argued, but cameras clicked and video buffs zoomed in on key scenes when, and *if* they managed to wheedle their way round Aaron Trent's acid tongue and his everlasting impatience.

'I want you to meet this guy…' He glanced now at Cass. 'I told you about him, didn't I? The expert? Bikes,' he explained, 'he knows all about bikes and racing, and I thought we needed somebody other than the riders themselves who are, to put it mildly, slightly prejudiced when it comes to asking who has the best, the fastest and the ton-up wonder.'

Cass grinned. 'All the lads like to think their bike is best,' she offered.

'I want that Teasdale one for the leader though.'

Cass nodded. 'He's one of the best, level-headed and dependable, but…'

'No "buts", baby. I want him, all right – but that bike of his just doesn't have the right image.' He stood gazing at the gleaming metal monster standing beside the war memorial. 'What do you think of that one?' His eyes narrowed against the sun. 'Think he'll take to it? Teasdale? D'you also think he's capable of holding on to something like that at speed?'

Cass followed his gaze with her own, and drew in her breath as she saw the model more closely. 'Hells-bells! He'll take to it like a duck to water. Dillon will be in Seventh Heaven riding a Harley Davidson.'

'You're sure?'

She nodded. 'I'm sure.'

'Well, as I said before, I want to introduce you to this new guy. I want you to get on with him. You understand,

Sandie? I need you to get on with him. In fact, I'm ordering you to get on with him. OK? I'm looking to you to make sure things run like clockwork around here. So be nice to him, will ya?'

'I get on with most folks. Even you – sometimes.'

He grabbed hold of her hand and hauled her across the market square. 'Hey,' he yelled as he came near the war memorial and one of the men swung a leg across the saddle of the bike and started up the engine, 'Hey – leave that for a minute guys... we have a problem.'

The man on the bike looked up and the volume of noise died down slightly.

'Jefferson! I need ya here.'

Behind her, the motorbike engine died altogether, and she heard two sets of footsteps coming over to them, but she couldn't be bothered now to think of introductions to the new man. She had to sort out the business of autumn leaves.

'Garden centres might be able to help you with the leaves,' she said. 'They'd know where to get things like artificial leaves. It's worth a try.'

Over her head, Trent roared, 'Jefferson, try garden centres. Sandie says garden centres have plastic leaves.'

Cass whirled round. Jefferson was Trent's side-kick. He took the blame for everything and usually managed to put things to rights when they invariably went wrong. Jefferson could be an angel, and Jefferson could also out-swear his boss when the need arose.

But it wasn't Jefferson that Cass's gaze was riveted on. It was the man beside him, striding out towards them across the square.

Her mouth dropped open, her legs turned to squidgy marshmallow. She managed a strangled, 'Oh, *h-e-ll*...!'

Trent yelled, 'Hi, Patric. Here's the little lady I was telling you about. Come and meet Sandie. Sandie's going to be real nice to you. You two – you're going to get along OK – I just know it.'

And before she knew it, her hand was jerked forward by the director and placed firmly in that of Patric Faulkner, who looked for all the world as if he'd just been confronted by a gunman about to pull the trigger.

'Are you sick or something?' Aaron Trent, never noted for tact, looked from one to the other as Patric let go of her hand as if it were a red hot iron and managed a strangled, 'Sandie? You're… *Sandie*…? The screenplay…'

'She wrote it all,' Trent ranted on, obviously irate. 'I told you about her, didn't I? Sure I told you about her.' He flapped his hands dismissively, 'You know darn well I told you we had this doll called Sandie who'd written the whole damn thing and was doing the screen-play.'

'Sandie!' Life was creeping back somehow into his iced-over veins. Patric Faulkner stared long and hard at her, and she seemed incapable of responding with even a 'Hi there!'

'Look – I've got see to Jefferson about them damn leaves.' Trent swung away from them and yelled to the man who was already twenty yards away from him and making for the nearest motorhome. 'Jefferson! Dammit. Wait, will you? I need those damn leaves, and I need them fast.'

'Sandie!' Patric said savagely. 'What does he mean by calling *you* 'Sandie'? I had no idea you were this "Sandie" person he kept going on about. What the hell's going on, Cass?'

Weakly she said, 'It was Trent's idea. He said he wanted to call me Sandie as it would sound good on the credits. I think he thought "Cassandra" was too long-winded and old-fashioned.'

'So you…'

'I went along with it. Where was the harm in it? Most people shorten my name to Cass anyway, but Trent wasn't keen on Cass.'

Irate he said, 'I never dreamed you'd be here. And, of course, I couldn't get hold of you by phone, even though I've tried ringing that damn mobile number you gave me till I was blue in the face. You always seem to have the thing switched off.'

'Not always.'

'Twenty-three hours and fifty-nine minutes out of every day then.' Sarcasm bit hard out of the anger he felt rising up inside him. 'I've been back to that place – Rydale whatever. Several times. You were never there though, so in desperation I went to Manchester to see if I could trace you…'

'I wasn't there either.'

Tersely he said, 'So I found out, after enquiring at all the damn newspaper offices and photographic places in the book. You seemed to have disappeared off the face of the earth, Cass.' He was staring intently at her face. 'For heaven's sake – why? What are you afraid of?'

'You had no right to try and trace me.' Stubborn and sullen-faced, she stood before him.

'I love you, Cass,' he said softly. 'You have no need to hide from me.'

'Perhaps not…' He detected a certain sadness in her face and began to relent a little.

'Cass,' he said in a more gentle tone than he'd used before. 'Cass – you can't wipe out the past just by changing your name.'

Her head came up sharply and he saw a warning in her eyes not to push her further. 'I told you – it was Trent's idea...not mine.'

'It *was* convenient for you, however. It put me off the scent.'

He saw her close her eyes momentarily as if she were either very confused or very weary. He felt sorry for her then. She'd done nothing wrong, so why was he treating her like she was a criminal? If he had to blame somebody for losing her, it should be himself. If only he'd started divorce proceedings earlier, they might have been together now.

She said, 'Don't try to get clever with me, Patric. This never should have happened. I had no idea you'd be involved with Aaron Trent over this television drama. If I *had* known...' The sentence hung there; she didn't seem to know how to finish it.

He felt he owed her some sort of explanation. 'Trent has an interest in the Cambridge racing circuit. He put a lot of money into the project and he's now on the board of directors. It was Trent who thought I could be of some use up here in Derbyshire, even though I don't know an awful lot about bike-racing. Cars are my special interest. I told him that. I'm glad now, though, that I let him persuade me to come here...'

'*I'm* not glad. This is awful, Patric.' She was glancing round now. 'I never imagined anything like this when you told me you were up in Derbyshire for a bit of business – just doing someone a favour, you said.'

'Aaron persuaded me to come up and look at the location with a view to advising on the bike scenes, even though I told him I didn't have much experience of motorbikes. Owning one in your teens and twenties doesn't make you an expert and I told him that. I was just somebody he knew though, and that was enough for him.'

'You told me Michelle would be joining you. Is she here?' Her eyes were suddenly tortured.

Gently he said, 'Yes. Although I left her at the bungalow today.'

"The bungalow". Talking about Michelle, he could see, was almost choking her.

'You still care, don't you?' He kept his voice low but knew she discerned the words even though there was shouting and movement all around them.

'No…' She looked round wildly as if she sought for some reason to rush away. Aaron Trent had disappeared though. Nobody had any use for her on the set just at that moment and he was relieved about that.

'You can't hide it, Cass. Don't even try to hide it or deny it. I know you still care. There was so much between us. You can't have forgotten.'

Her face flamed. 'I *have* to forget. There's no point in remembering. We don't have a future.'

'I won't let you forget.'

Her head jerked up again. 'Why are you doing this?' Pain was etched on her features, in her eyes, it caught in her voice and stilled him. It was no use reminding her of what was past. Nothing was any use now, nor would it be ever again. She was right. They had no future. He'd lost her. She'd told him that day in Rydale Tor that she'd found somebody else. He had to accept that.

He backed away a step. 'Cass…I'm sorry, but us meeting up again like this… It surely must mean something to you?'

'We can *only* be friends.' At last she spoke with some-thing in her voice that made him remember the old Cass – the sensible and practical and down-to-earth Cass he had loved. *Still loved*, he vowed to himself. Nothing could ever kill that love. Nothing could ever make him walk away and forget her.

'I have work to do.' She half-turned away, her gaze scanning the trucks, the huts and the motorhomes.

His hand was on her arm now. Detaining her for just a moment longer. He had to know. He had to ask her again. She'd said, that day in Rydale Tor, that there was somebody else in her life now but still he had to be sure about that.

'Cass – you told me there was somebody else in your life. It wasn't true, was it…? Tell me it wasn't true. It's important I should know. If I thought you'd found somebody else, I don't know if I could bear it…'

His voice was drowned by a sudden surge of noise as a dozen bikes came roaring down the hill into the market square. Cass shook his hand away from her and put both her own hands up to her ears to shut out the din.

'Hell!' He swore softly under his breath. 'Can't we get some peace and quiet round here for a few minutes?'

The motorbikes, all powerful ones, all different colours, different makes, gaudy, iridescent green, pink, red, silver, black, roared into the square, lining up neatly – all except one.

That one came speeding over to where they stood, circled them as it slowed down, then with a thunderous revving of its engine came to a standstill beside them. Patric watched as the rider steadied the huge machine with one black-booted foot planted squarely on the ground.

He was wearing black leathers and a black-and-gold helmet which, with his gloved hands, he was slowly removing.. He had eyes for nobody but Cass, Patric saw with an overwhelming ache dragging at his heart. The rider had laughing blue eyes and a shock of blond hair through which he raked his fingers so that it stood on end. The high leather close-fitting collar of the riding suit made the perfect foil for that blond hair.

Patric felt uneasy as he watched her spring eagerly towards the bike, almost as if she welcomed the interruption.

The blonde biker said casually, 'Hi, Cass!'

'Dillon.'

Patric saw the man glance at him before asking her, 'Are you going to introduce me?'

'Sure.' She smiled.

Patric looked at first one and then the other as she made the introductions, and he felt a slow and steady hatred creeping into his heart. Dillon Teasdale seemed to know her well. They were laughing together now. Joking. Some stupid joke about a Honda Goldwing. He didn't want to listen, didn't want to hear her laughing with some other man. She didn't laugh with *him* any more, and they'd had lots of laughs together in the old days…

'You can forget the Goldwing now. You'll have a bike equal to the Goldwing,' she was saying.

'You mean it?' The blond man's face was animated. He looked just like a kid, Patric thought. She'd taken up with a kid. He felt sick and angry and humiliated because she'd chosen someone so different to what he was himself, someone so young. A bike freak. He couldn't stand this.

She was nodding. 'It's over by the war memorial. Aaron Trent wants you to take the lead.'

He glanced towards the war memorial, saw the bike and recognised the make. His mouth dropped open, then he muttered in a hoarse voice, 'On a Harley? You're not kidding me, Cass? Trent wants me on the Harley?'

She shook her head. 'I wouldn't kid you about something

so important to you.' She was laughing again.

Damn her! Damn her to hell! Patric felt like hitting out at the man who could make her laugh. She was so relaxed with the blond biker. So…so familiar. Brutally, he thought, it hadn't taken her long to forget…

'It's true, Dillon. Trent told me himself. He wants you as leader – on the Harley-Davidson.'

'You pulled strings for me?'

'No. I only said you were a good rider…'

'You did it for *me*, Cass?'

'You're the best rider, Dillon. You know you are – and the most enthusiastic.'

'Cass!' The man on the bike grabbed her, pulled her towards him, kissed her full on the lips, then as she reeled back breathless he yelled, 'I've just got to tell the gang!'. Jamming the helmet back on his head, he kicked the engine into life and the bike roared away again.

Patric held himself rigidly in check, knowing if once he let his anger free, it would be the end of everything they'd ever had between them.

'So,' he said menacingly. 'That's the lie of the land, is it? Dillon Teasdale – leader of the pack.'

She stared at him. She was breathing heavily. 'I don't know what you mean?'

'Oh, I think you do.' Stubborn pride made him force an uncaring note into his voice. He wanted to hurt her, because inside he was hurting so much himself. He wouldn't let her know that though. Mistakenly, he believed that would be a sign of weakness.

'You know damn well,' he added. 'I was asking you about that somebody else you hinted at the other week. It now seems as if I have no need to ask. The question is answered for me, isn't it? That somebody else is a damned

Hells Angel – Dillon Teasdale!'

Unable to bear being near her any longer, he spun around on his heels and strode off purposefully across the square again and, as he left her, he forced himself to ignore the small voice that followed him.

'He's not a Hells Angel! Patric…listen to me…you don't understand!'

But Patric was beyond listening, he was so full of anger.

chapter six

Cass lived on a knife-edge for the rest of the morning, dreading to meet up with Patric again.

Seeing him had unsettled her. She'd had no idea he was involved with Aaron Trent and had thought herself safe from him. Now, though, her mind was filled with foreboding. How was she going to be able to avoid him when they'd be working so closely together? And, more to the point, how on earth was she going to keep baby Tiffany a secret from him?

Luckily, Trent knew nothing about the baby so from that quarter there was no threat; *he* wouldn't be letting anything slip about her private life to Patric. As she tucked the film script firmly under her arm, she was determined to keep her mind on her work which was all important to her at the moment. There'd be time enough after filming had finished for the day in which to let her mind dwell on Patric.

She perched herself on a low dry stone wall outside the local 'Lead-Miner' pub, well out of camera reach, and watched the motorbike shots getting underway, first of all the whole gang of twenty plus, congregating in an untidy mass in the market square, and then Dillon on his own, roaring up on the Harley to join them with an enthusiasm that brought a smile to her face.

Trent had chosen him as leader and she knew he'd made a good choice. Dillon was a natural with bikes. She watched Trent who was relaxed, capable and in charge of things, some distance away from her. He and Dillon got on well, they'd hit it off from the first moment they'd met. Dillon was easy going though; she knew that from past experience of him working on the electrics in her photographic studio. He might well be a 'jack-the-lad' but he had a rakish, jokey personality, and was well-liked by the other bikers.

If Trent said 'jump' – Dillon jumped, and in all the right places and at all the right times. If Trent said 'Ride like the wind' that's exactly what he did. Dillon had a capacity for keeping a clear head at all times, and also an aptitude for becoming not just a rider, but a vital part of the bike itself. The Harley responded to him, came alive under him. It sometimes seemed to Cass that the reason for Dillon's existence on earth was to ride.

His conversations revolved around 'centrifugal forces,' 'centres of gravity', and 'frictional resistance'! They were natural-born words to him; words that he understood implicitly, words that excited him and brought a light into his eyes and a reverence to his voice every time he uttered them.

Trent was yelling now, 'Everybody back in their places – I want the Harley for a close up.'

The bikers backed off, drifted away as the cameras closed in on a back view of Dillon.

Cass hoped it wouldn't take long. She needed to talk to Dillon. She wasn't wanted here at the moment, however, so she hopped down from the wall and went inside the pub. She ordered two drinks, paid for them and took them to a table near the door. It was half-past twelve. They'd be breaking for lunch any time now. She didn't know where Patric was; he seemed to have disappeared and she was thankful for that.

Dillon came in twenty minutes later and sat down opposite her.

'I got you a shandy. Is that okay?' She glanced up over the rim of her own glass. 'I hope it hasn't gone flat.'

'If it's cool and wet, it'll be perfect!' He drank thirstily and grinned at her. 'That's it for the day. I'm getting back home after this. Do you want a lift?'

She shook her head and laughed. 'I came in the car. Anyway, I don't have a crash helmet.'

'You bring the car so you can get back to Tiff in a hurry if you have to, don't you? I could give you a lift here and back most days if it weren't for that.'

She grimaced slightly. 'Am I such a worrier about her? Does it show? I hope I'm not turning into one of those "clingy" sort of women.'

'She's perfectly all right, you know. Greer Stuart has really taken to her, and Greer loves kids.'

Cass sighed. 'I guess I'm still too much of a new mummy to be able to relax when Tiff's out of my sight, even knowing that Greer is very capable. Right now though, Dill – I need to ask you a favour.'

'Fire away.' He leaned back, crossed his black-booted ankles and looked at her through lazy eyes.

'I don't want you to mention Tiff. Not to anybody here on the set, not even to Trent. My private life is just that, private, and I want to keep it that way.'

His shoulders lifted in a shrug. 'Why would I want to talk about Tiff – to Trent or anyone else, Cass?'

She knew she would have to explain. 'Look – I know you don't gossip, but *somebody* might just start making enquiries about me,' she said, swirling the liquid around in her glass and looking down at it, not at him.

'Somebody?'

She glanced up to find he was gazing at her in a quizzical manner.

'Not the guy you introduced me to this morning, by any chance?' he asked, narrowing his eyes at her as the truth dawned.

Cass felt her face flushing. 'Patric Faulkner – yes,' she said. 'I don't want him to know about Tiff, Dillon.'

'I think I can guess why you don't want Tiff mentioned to *him*,' Dillon said, his voice steady. 'Tiff's the spitting image of him. Am I on the right track, Cass?'

'Hell! Is it so obvious?'

'I put two and two together,' he admitted. 'You were decidedly jittery this morning with that guy and when I gave you that hug, he looked as if he might just about murder me. And then I got to wondering where I'd seen him before, but it took me some time to connect him with Tiff. All that dark hair and eyes, and a certain way of looking at you that Tiff has. She's Faulkner in miniature. There's no doubting that little darling's parentage!'

'She looks like him, I know,' Cass admitted. 'But I don't want Patric to find out about her. It would only complicate matters at the moment – and just as I'm getting my life together nicely. The past is past and I don't want it to be raked up again. Do you understand?'

Dillon shook his head at her. 'You're crazy. The minute he sets eyes on her, he'll know that she's his kid.'

'He's not going to see her. Not ever.' Her words were passionate. 'He must never do that.'

Dillon sat forward in his seat, rested his clasped hands on the table and stared across at her. 'Don't you think he has a *right* to know that he has a baby daughter?'

Taking a deep breath, she said, 'His ex-wife's still dependent upon him.'

For a second she saw shock in his eyes. Then he said, 'So! That's it, is it? It figures that you don't want him to know – him *or* his wife, I take it. Tiff doesn't get a ready-made daddy just yet then?'

She shook her head. 'No chance of that Dill. None at all!'

'No hope of you and him setting up house all nice and cosy, like?'

'Not the faintest hope of us getting together,' she said firmly.

'Why not?'

'His wife's…' she paused, 'Michelle had an accident that left her in a wheel chair. He couldn't possibly desert her entirely.'

'And the bastard didn't tell you he had a wife, I suppose.'

'I *knew* he had a wife, Dillon, but he was divorced from her before I found myself pregnant with Tiff. I can't make any excuses for either myself *or* for Patric. It was just something that happened – something that *had* to happen, if you know what I mean. We were in love and everything looked as if it was going to be OK for us. And then Michelle had a dreadful accident…'

For a moment she saw a look of absolute disbelief flit across his face, before he muttered, 'Cass – I can hardly believe that you…'

'Split them up?' She gave a feeble little laugh. 'It wasn't like that. He was in the process of getting divorced when I met him. She had someone else too at the time. It was all supposed to work out perfectly, but…' She gave a heavy sigh. 'These things don't work out, do they? Not when you're depending on them to do so.'

'I take it that the *someone else* doesn't want her?'

'He died.'

'So – back to the faithful hubby? Or ought I to say "*faithless*" hubby?' There was a look of hurt surprise in his eyes. Obviously, Cass thought, Dillon had never expected this of her.

Wearily she said, 'He wasn't unfaithful to her. Anyway, it's a long story, Dillon.' In a matter-of-fact manner, she proceeded to give him the barest details about Michelle and what had happened in the past without dramatising or exaggerating the truth in any way. At last she said, 'Michelle can be dangerous, and maybe I oughtn't to be telling you all this, but you *are* connected to *me*, and Michelle's the sort of woman who will exploit every situation to suit herself. She might even try getting at you to hurt me. But I'm not going to give her the chance if I can help it.'

Stunned, Dillon stared at her. 'Wowee!' he said at last. 'With a past like you have, lady, I'm not surprised that you can come up with amazing fiction, like the film we're seeing come to life here.'

'That was pure imagination.' She managed a laugh. 'Trent asked me to write something up-to-date, but with undertones of a true story about two lovers who were parted in the 1600's when the plague came to Derbyshire.'

He shrugged. 'A lot of the bikers know you've got a baby,' he said. 'Are you going to silence the lot of them? They've seen her, remember? They come along to Rydale Tor every Sunday afternoon. They park their bikes right outside your window. They pretend they're great big tough guys at times, but when either you, or Greer, walks by with Tiff in the buggy, they all go soft and make cooey-gooey noises at her, and pull daft faces.'

'They bring her little teddy bears and things that rattle, too.' Her laugh was shaky. 'One of them even presented her with an ice-lolly last weekend.'

'Greer told me about that – said she had to eat it herself, and they all cheered her.'

'I heard the racket from upstairs,' Cass said, smiling.

Dillon sobered. 'They won't mention the baby to anybody if I tell them not to,' he said at last. 'Do you want me to do that, Cass? Have a word with them?'

'Please.' She fiddled with her fingers on the table top. 'It would only complicate matters even further if Patric ever found out he had a daughter, but I don't want gossip to start up about Patric and Michelle.'

'There's no need for the lads to know *all* the details,' he said, as a commotion broke out beyond the door and some of the bikers pushed their way inside and made for the bar, shouting for shandies and that other Derbyshire delicacy – the chip-cob. One turned and looked at Cass, lifted a hand and yelled, 'When are you going to bring the tot to see us being made into movie stars, love?'

'Oh, no…' Cass breathed.

Dillon was on his feet in seconds. He grinned down at her. 'Leave it to me,' he said. 'You get off home now. I'll see to this lot for you.'

'Thanks.' She pushed herself to her feet. 'I'll see you later perhaps.'

As he moved away he said, 'I'm picking Greer up later. She lives quite near where I live with Mam. See you then – and Cass, don't worry. We'll sort this out between us, huh?'

Outside in the fresh air, she saw that filming had come to a stop. The crew were sitting around, eating sandwiches on motorhome steps, lounging against walls. Most of the onlookers had drifted away. They'd be back though. Trent's big car was nowhere to be seen and she was glad of that. Wherever Trent was, she could guess that Patric was with him.

She made her way over to where she'd left her car, got into it quickly, and drove out of the village towards home.

chapter seven

Michelle Faulkner drove slowly along the High Street of Rydale Tor in her car, taking note of house numbers, shop signs and such. She knew exactly what she was looking for. She had a detailed report on the seat beside her, telling her where Cass lived, who her neighbours were, and stating also that Cass had a child – a little girl a few months old. She had paid a high price for the information but she didn't regret the expense.

Eventually locating the empty shop with the side entrance to Cass's flat, she pulled her car over onto the river side of the road opposite and parked. With her disability-scheme parking badge she wouldn't be moved on, even though parking was restricted in some parts of the centre of town.

She sat and watched the flat for maybe ten minutes, eventually coming to the conclusion that nobody was at home. Then, just as she was about to move on, a gauzy curtain upstairs was swished back and a girl stood there with a baby in her arms.

At first, Michelle thought the girl was pointing at her car, but then she realised she must be pointing at the ducks on the river, for the baby began flapping its arms up and down and jigging in the girl's arms.

But the girl wasn't Cass Fairburn.

Michelle checked the details on the sheet beside her again. It was definitely the right address. And there was a baby there – and a little girl baby by the look of things because it was dressed in something pink and fluffy – an all-in-one-suit of some sort.

The curtain dropped into place again and Michelle sat, tense, holding her breath. There was a pain deep inside her, a deep-seated longing to hold a baby in her arms just as that girl at the window had been holding the child. She wondered what its name was. The private investigator had obviously thought a baby's name was unimportant.

Michelle felt bereft. And then anger surged inside her. She should be the one holding a baby. And if it hadn't been for her hot-headedness in racing away in the car after she'd hit Craig with it – and killed him – she might now, at this moment, be holding Craig's child in *her* arms.

She lost the baby though in the subsequent accident when she'd gone through a red light – apparently without seeing it. It was all a blur in her mind now – the pain, the drifting in and out of consciousness, the long struggle to stand on her own two feet again. In hospital, they'd broken the news of her miscarriage carefully, and at the time it hadn't bothered her all that much because in reality she was less than two months gone and she hadn't even known she was pregnant.

Afterwards, though, when she remembered what she'd done to Craig – rammed the car at him because she thought he'd been unfaithful to her – and she knew with a dreadful finality that she'd never see him again, that was when she started to hanker after something as a living reminder of the affair.

And then to find out that Cass Fairburn had a baby – and Patric's baby at that – was the final humiliation.

She clenched her hands tightly on the steering wheel of the car and kept her gaze fixed firmly on that window above the empty shop. Hatred flared, not against the baby, but against Cass herself because Cass had something lasting to treasure. And it wasn't fair! She realised now that she should have hung on to Patric herself. She should have stayed faithful to him while she had the chance. But maybe there was still hope…?

Even as such thoughts flitted in and out of her mind, Michelle knew that she needed to keep her wits about her. Patric had never strayed in all the years of their marriage. Not until it was obvious that the marriage had nothing more going for it – and not until she herself had been unfaithful to him and the divorce was finalised.

Michelle felt stifled in the car. Outside the sun was shining and there was a stiff May breeze rippling the shallows of the river. She inched herself out of the car. It was difficult with legs that wouldn't always obey her; bones that clicked and creaked like those of an old woman of ninety. But movement was easier now she'd taken to wearing trousers out of doors, instead of a skirt. Her knees were swollen, her feet sore from the pressure of her shoes, but she had fought to regain some normality and though it had taken over a year, she could stand with dignity now and walk in a shuffling awkward manner with the help of crutches. The wheelchair she despised, hating it with a vehemence that could and had, in the past, reduced her to a shambling heap of tears and tantrums. The wheelchair was a reminder of all she had lost, all she recoiled from. It was her penance for killing a man, her conscience too for losing the baby through her own actions. She had been driving too fast that night – and had been reckless beyond all comprehension. It wasn't Craig she dreamed about and had nightmares about however; it was the loss of everything she'd had before – the good life, the dancing and parties.

She slammed the car door, not bothering to lock it, because she had no intention of moving far away from it. There were benches all along the promenade beside the river and she hobbled her way to the nearest and sat down, breathless and full of pain. It took her several minutes to compose herself, then she delved into her pocket, took out a small brown pill bottle and shook two painkillers into her hand. She swallowed them easily. It had become habit just lately. She didn't even need a glass of water nowadays. When the pain got bad in her legs…well, she argued to herself, it was worth it, just to stand up and to be able to shuffle. Nothing would induce her to rely on that damned wheelchair again.

The pills began to work almost immediately. They were from her consultant at the hospital and they were strong. She remembered him saying, 'Not too many now. They'll rot your liver!' But he'd smiled as he said it and she'd assured him that she was an intelligent woman and, as such, would never misuse his drugs.

She could see Cass Fairburn's flat from here and it wasn't long before the side door opened and a buggy was being pushed out.

She sat up then, fighting the grogginess the pills always brought on, and watched with interest as the girl pushed the buggy to the edge of the pavement, waited till the road was clear, and then came straight across to the riverside.

Michelle's excitement mounted. Her eyes sought out the child in the buggy as they came nearer – it was, as she'd assumed, a little girl. And it was Patric's baby – there was no mistaking that. She felt no animosity towards the child. Quite the contrary. She smiled as the girl pushed the buggy across the promenade – no more that a couple of metres away from her now, and the baby smiled back at her with

Patric's mouth tilting twistedly, Patric's dark eyes lighting up, and Patric's charm apparent in her baby-hands reaching out towards her. It was Patric as he'd been when she first knew him years ago. Patric when he'd been young and free and life hadn't thrown a whole load of dross at him – in the shape of a wife who had deceived him.

Realising now, perhaps for the first time, how much she had lost when she had played around with Craig Andrews, Michelle knew only one thing. She wanted that baby – or *a* baby. Nothing else would do. Looking at Patric's child, she realised that Cass had something that she, Michelle, could never have, and Michelle didn't like that thought one little bit.

The girl swivelled the buggy round and made for the bench.

'Do you mind if we sit here?'

Michelle said, 'No, not all. Please do. Here, let me move these crutches – they're a nuisance…' She grabbed at the metal crutches and pushed them over the back of the seat. They dropped with a clang on the hard concrete.

The baby squealed with delight at the noise and began battering the apron front of the buggy with her tiny hands.

The girl laughed and sat down, pulling the buggy up near herself and away from Michelle.

'What's her name?' Michelle felt bound to ask the question. She felt she had a right to know. This was, after all, her own husband's baby.

'Tiffany?' The girl smiled. 'Tiff for short. She's gorgeous, isn't she?'

'Is she yours?'

The girl shook her head. 'I'm her nanny.'

'Oh! Mummy works, does she?'

The girl smiled again but didn't answer. Obviously,

Michelle thought, she was a model employee who didn't discuss other people's business.

'We come to feed the ducks most days.' The girl leaned forward. 'Don't we, Tiff?'

The baby clapped her hands.

'She has such tiny fingers.' Michelle was captivated by the baby.

'They're lovely at this age.' The girl nodded.

'Do you like being a nanny?'

The girl nodded again. 'I love it.'

'Yet with your looks – and that red-gold hair, you could be anything you wanted to be,' Michelle said.

'I am what I want to be.' The girl gave a little shrug. 'I love kiddies.'

'You are so pretty though.'

The girl flushed. 'I think we ought to be getting back…'

'No. Don't go. I didn't mean to be rude.'

'You weren't being rude.'

'What do they call you? What is your name?'

'Greer.' The girl seemed uncomfortable.

'A lovely name. There was once a film star called Greer – and she was beautiful.'

'Yes. I know. People always tell me.'

'Till it gets a bore.'

The girl said, 'Well, yes. I suppose so.'

'Would you do something for me?' An idea had come to Michelle.

Greer frowned. 'If I can.'

'There's a folding wheelchair in the boot of my car. Would you get it for me?'

'Now?'

Michelle nodded.

'I…er…'

'I'd keep an eye on the baby for you. It would be a plea-sure.'

Greer shook her head. 'I'll take her with me.' She held out her hand. 'Will you give me your car keys?'

Michelle handed over the keys. 'You really can leave this little darling with me. She'll be quite safe.'

Greer hung onto the handle of the buggy. 'No. I'll take her with me.'

Michelle watched as the girl put the brake on the buggy beside her car, watched too while Greer took the wheelchair out of the boot of the car and opened it up and made it stable.

She closed the boot up and locked it, and came back wheeling the buggy with one hand, the wheelchair with the other. When the wheelchair was beside Michelle, Greer asked if she wanted help getting into it.

'Oh, I'm not going to get into it,' Michelle replied.

'Oh.' Greer sat down on the bench again, positioned the buggy right against herself, and handed the keys back to Michelle.

'Thank you. Do you think you could reach the crutches now, my dear?'

Greer slipped a hand between the seat and the back rails and retrieved the crutches.

'Thank you.' Michelle hoisted herself to her feet and balanced delicately before daring to move her feet.

Michelle could sense the girl watching her as she turned to the wheelchair and pulled it round in front of her. Then, with much painful dragging of her feet and pushing the wheelchair, she went right to the edge of the river bank and tipped the chair into the fast flowing water.

Ducks set up a furious squawking and she heard Greer cry out, 'Oh, no! Oh, no! Don't jump in…'

Michelle swung round after making sure that the wheelchair was being carried far out into the middle of the rushing water. She had a smile on her lips, as she faced Greer. 'I'm not going to jump,' she said, 'You silly girl.'

There was a frozen look of horror on Greer's face as she stood hanging on to the buggy, not daring to move.

Michelle shuffled back toward the bench, then just stood there and said, 'I've wanted to do that for a long, long time. It was redundant. It's time I made a more positive effort to walk everywhere and not rely on that thing.'

Greer just shook her head. She was speechless.

'And you know something else?'

Greer, still not uttering a word, shook her head.'

'I'm going to have a baby.'

'Oh!'

'Yes. I really am. I'm going to have a baby – by any means possible. I have decided! I think I deserve one.'

And with the words, she turned away and went back to the car.

When Patric came in at eight o'clock, she'd had a whole afternoon in which to wonder how to deal with the situation that had sprung up. Now she had evidence that Patric had come here for a reason. Now that she had seen the baby for herself. Now she knew that Cass Fairburn was still on the scene.

But did *he* know all those things? And if he didn't, how could she tell him about them without giving away the fact that she'd actually hired somebody to find out the girl's whereabouts?

A sickening feeling of disgust came over her whenever she allowed herself to remember that balding, greasy little man in his plush office, whom she'd paid to find Cass Fairburn for her. She'd been driven to it, she convinced herself. She'd suspected, however, when Patric had first mentioned Derbyshire, that there was an ulterior motive behind him coming here. And she'd been proven right.

He called out to her from the hall. 'Michelle! Do you want your car garaging?'

She didn't answer. Under her breath she muttered, 'Come in here to speak to me. Don't yell me from the front door as if I were a dog being summoned to lick your boots.'

She heard his footsteps coming down the tiled hall. He pushed the door open.

'Didn't you hear me come in?'

She'd never been a woman who played her hand cagily. 'Of course I heard you.'

'Well, do you want your car garaging?' He stood in the doorway as she faced him from her seat beside the hearth.

'No. It's perfectly all right where it is. You know it's awkward for me. That damned little garage is far too small. And if I want to go out – I'll go. I don't need to ask your permission, or say "Please, darling, will you get the car out for me".' She was sitting in an easy chair with a glass of whisky on a small table beside her. She slammed a hand down on the chair arm. 'I will not be treated like a child.'

'I don't treat you like a child.' He went into the room, walked over to a cabinet and pulled out a metal box. Cigarettes lay piled there in neat rows as he opened it, but he snapped it shut again without taking one.

'Still resisting the urge?' she asked in a sneering tone of voice.

'It gets easier.' He smiled at her.

'You still have the odd one.'

He shrugged his broad shoulders. 'It's better than before.'

'You were easier to live with when you were a twenty-a-day man.'

'I don't doubt it. They dulled my senses.'

She could tell he was not going to be drawn into yet another argument. He smiled pleasantly at her – as if she were a stranger he'd just met, she thought pettishly.

'Have you had a good day? Did you get out on the moors as you'd planned?'

'I always do exactly as I plan,' she said, making her voice bitter.

'Good.' He sat down in a low chair and stuck out his long legs, crossing his ankles easily. He leaned his head back against the cushions.

'How much longer?' she wanted to know. 'How long before this damn film is finished?'

'Trent won't need me once the motorbike sequences are done.'

'Which is – when?' Her chin came up in a determined manner. She wouldn't rest until they were back in Suffolk, for good.

He moved his shoulders easily. 'Another few weeks. It depends on the weather to some extent.'

'Weeks?' Her voice was a shriek. 'We are *not* staying here for endless weeks, surely? Hell! I shall go mad with boredom.'

'You can always go back home…'

'You'd like that,' she snapped, cutting him off in mid sentence.

He didn't argue with her on that score. He just said, 'Look – don't blame me. *You're* the one who's bored with this place.'

'While you…' She bit on her lip. It wouldn't do to start slinging allegations at him – not just yet. She had to bide her time. She had to know just where she stood.

'It makes a change for me – a change from the race circuit. I'm quite enjoying this bracing fresh air and the outdoor life. No board meetings, no cushy office and cups of coffee every half hour.'

'You look disgustingly healthy,' she said, scowling.

'I like it here and the scenery is out of this world – so green and wide open.'

'I *hate* it.'

'Go home then. Go back to Suffolk. Nobody's forcing you to stay in Derbyshire.'

A sudden thought struck her. 'No – I'll come to the film set. That might make things a bit more bearable.'

'You'd hate that too. You'd hate everything about it, the noise, the fumes from the bikes, the wires waiting to trip you up all over the place. It would bore you silly,' he said.

'You patronising rat!'

He got up from the chair. 'I'm going to have a shower.'

'You never talk to me.'

'We have nothing to say to each other any more, Michelle.'

'You loved me once,' she spat out.

He stopped, halfway to the door, turned and faced her. 'Yes,' he agreed. 'I did – once. And I thought then that the feeling was returned – that I was all you wanted. It wasn't enough though, was it – marriage?'

Softening her voice a little, she said, 'We could go back to what we were…' Uncertainty made her falter. She'd never spoken to him like this before. It was difficult, but there was a lot at stake. If he found out that Cass Fairburn had given birth to his baby, a crippled ex-wife would stand no chance at all of holding on to him.

He laughed in her face. 'What's your game this time?'

he asked in a biting tone. 'What's behind this sudden surge of happy-ever-after?'

'We used to be happy.' Her voice had lost its bitterness now.

'Did we?'

It was unexpected – that note of derision in his voice. Usually he tried to placate her. Now, all of a sudden, he seemed not to care one way or another whether he antagonised her or not.

'Don't you want me on the film set?'

'No,' he said without a moment's hesitation. 'No, I don't want you there.'

'Why not?' Her hands fell into her lap and clasped themselves tightly together.

He gave a heavy sigh then said, 'You might as well know now as later. Cass Fairburn's there. She wrote the screenplay. And before you ask – no, I didn't know she'd be there. It came as a shock to me when Trent introduced us.'

She swallowed her anger and made her voice pleasant. 'You still care for her, I suppose.'

'Yes,' he said. 'I do. Now, are there any other questions before I take that shower?'

She averted her head and didn't answer. When she looked round again, he'd gone. She was breathing heavily. He didn't know about the baby, of that she was sure. He'd have told her if he did.

She smiled to herself. It was her secret. Hers and Cass Fairburn's. It seemed that neither of them wanted him to know about the baby.

Bargains could be struck, she decided, knowing that Cass must surely realise now how dangerous an adversary she could be? Especially when the girl looking after Tiffany told her about today's little incident on the river bank.

There was hope, she told herself, that she'd win him back. She had the upper hand. *She'd* once been his wife and that was as good a starting point as any. And while they were here in Derbyshire, he was still living under the same roof with her, and she'd be damned if she'd give him up easily to that little witch who'd ensnared him when he was at his most vulnerable!

chapter eight

Greer was kneeling beside the big bath, bathing Tiffany, who was surrounded by yellow plastic ducks when Cass got home around half-past-five that night.

'Hi! I tried not to be late. Dillon said he'd be calling to take you home.' Cass skipped round Greer, bent over the bath and dropped a kiss on Tiff's head. 'Hi, poppet,' she whispered. 'What have you been doing today?'

'Feeding the ducks.' Greer looked up solemnly at Cass and then continued, 'And something very sinister happened – something I want to tell you about after this little bundle is in bed.'

Cass felt jittery. 'Sinister?'

'Don't get all worried,' Greer said in her most practical tone of voice. 'But it's something I think you should know about. You might be able to throw more light on it than I can. You might even know the woman concerned. I'd certainly never seen her before in my life, but…'

'Woman!' Cass had a feeling of impending doom. 'What woman, Greer?'

Greer was busy soaping Tiffany and squeezing a sponge over her tummy, making the baby giggle and squeal. She looked up into Cass's face. 'She walked with crutches, but she had a wheelchair in the boot of her car.'

'A wheelchair!' Cass felt paralysed with shock. She knew of only one woman who used a wheelchair.

'A stranger to the place,' Greer was saying now. 'But you'll never guess what she did. She pushed the wheelchair into the river, and just watched it being carried away.'

'Oh, no.' Cass knew she had turned white. She felt like her legs would buckle under her too at any minute now.

'She didn't seem to care. And then she just got up and said the strangest thing.'

Cass stood and waited.

'Look,' Greer said, 'I'll give Dillon a call on his mobile and tell him I'm staying on awhile, shall I? For some reason I think what happened this afternoon was important and I think you should know all about it. You see, the woman, she said she was going to have a baby – by any means possible – and the way she looked at Tiff – well, it just scared me.'

Cass worried for half the next day whether to tell Patric about what had happened in Rydale the day before. Things were hotting up as far as the film was concerned, and she didn't have much time to look for him – but plenty of time to stew, and to wonder whether she ought to mention her fears to him or not.

To tell him that Michelle had obviously found out about her would inevitably mean telling Patric about Tiffany too. But if Michelle now knew about Tiffany, surely she would have wasted no time in telling him about the daughter he didn't know existed.

It was a problem without an answer. Dillon took her mind off it to some extent by larking about with some of the lads, and then whizzing over to her on the Harley-Davidson.

'How about a ride, Cass? You did, after all, land me this plum job.'

'Some job,' she retaliated. 'You're loving every minute of it – it's more like a vacation to you, not a job.'

'Dead right!' He grinned. 'You're not getting any hassle

from Mister flippin' Faulkner though, are you, Cass?'

'Not so you'd notice.' She pulled a face at him and looking over his shoulder as he sat on the bike in front of her, went on, 'He is however, at this very moment, striding across the market square towards us – and with a face like a thundercloud.'

Dillon made a huge show of swatting the back of his neck with one leather-gloved hand. 'I thought I could feel daggers hitting me in the back.' He pulled a wry face. 'I'd better be off.'

Patric, near enough to be heard now, yelled, 'Trent's looking for you, Teasdale. They're doing the moors scene this afternoon and he wants to brief you about it.'

Dillon saluted smartly and said so only Cass could hear, 'Aye-aye, Cap'n.'

She spluttered with laughter as Dillon roared off on the Harley and Patric came up to her, asking in a cool voice, 'Did I say something funny?'

'You did rather sound like a sergeant major. Or, as Dillon saw it, the captain of the ship,' she said, her voice teasing.

She saw him stiffen. 'You didn't get your customary hug before he left you, I noticed. Was that because I was around?'

'Customary hug, huh? Interesting!' She raised an enquiring eyebrow.

'It seemed as if you were well used to it the last time. It didn't faze you any. I assumed it was something you were used to.'

'Don't be so stuffy and out-of-touch,' she said. She longed to have him back as he'd been in the past – friendly, loving, approachable and caring.

He seemed to retreat into himself even further, however, thrusting his hands into the pockets of his short leather jacket and staring belligerently at her. 'You've changed,' he said. 'You're not the girl I once knew.'

'I've grown up,' she replied, leaning against a stone wall, totally relaxed, with the sun full on her as she lifted her face for its caress.

'You've certainly done that. You're making quite a name for yourself. You'll be famous when this film is finished.'

'Mmm. Maybe. It would be nice. But it was just a challenge that Trent threw out to me. We met on a picture shoot I was doing in London…'

'You fell on your feet – mere challenge or not,' he said stiffly. 'Good for you.'

Quick as a shot she came back at him, 'Don't be such a hypocrite, Patric. I take it you're miffed about something so say what you mean, will you?'

'I liked you as you used to be.'

Not able to stop herself, she snapped, 'And how was that? Available? Is that how you liked me? Always there for you? A nice comfy cushion you could turn to when things were hurting?'

If she'd hit him full in the face he couldn't have looked more hurt or surprised. 'Cass,' he said softly, 'That was unfair. I didn't use you. I thought you loved me as much as I loved you.'

She realised she shouldn't have said what she did. Yesterday's incident though had un-nerved her. If Michelle could toss a wheelchair into a fast-flowing river, how much more easier it would it be to toss Tiffany in too – if she got the chance? Cass was frightened but she thawed a little towards Patric, who knew nothing of what had happened in Rydale yesterday.

'I'm sorry,' she said, 'But this is stupid – each of us avoiding one another, and being over-polite or else sarcastic every time we meet. Filming will soon be over and we can go our separate ways, but we aren't being fair to Aaron Trent, acting the way we are towards one another.'

He came and hoisted himself up on to the wall beside where she was leaning. He stayed quiet and never spoke. She glanced at him and saw he was gazing around at the spectacular views that surrounded the village – scenes that from all angles were proving to be dramatic backdrops for the film. One aspect was high, dark moorland above the pretty peak district village, and it was from here that one of the three roads that converged on the village centre dropped steeply down to the market place. A second road came rambling in from rich pasture land to the left of them, and a third twisted and turned through a high-sided, rock-walled valley.

Cass was looking now at the pasture land – at cows in fields and twelve-week-old lambs finding their feet and no longer following closely at their mothers' heels. She was looking and wondering and thinking about Tiffany who was back home with Greer taking care of her. She wasn't quite so worried about Michelle now; she knew instinctively that after telling Greer the whole story about herself and Patric – Michelle's husband – Greer would take no chances.

'How is Michelle?' she asked in a practical voice. 'Does she like Derbyshire now that she's up here with you?'

'She hates it.' He was looking away from her. 'She's able to drive again now and walk a little bit with crutches. She gets out most days, shopping mainly, I think. She never tells me where she's been.' His voice was flat and devoid of emotion. He turned his head slowly and looked at her. 'You're not interested in Michelle,' he said, 'and neither am I. You know that, Cass. You know damn well there's nothing left of what Michelle and I once meant to each other.'

Quietly and with genuine feeling, she said, 'Is it really no better, Patric?'

'It never will be. It was over a long time ago. You knew that.'

'But I thought – with Michelle needing you so much now...'

He said, 'I don't actually live with her, you know. She has a live-in housekeeper and a nurse back home. I moved out, into a small flat nearby. She doesn't need me. She doesn't need anybody. She's still the same old Michelle – heartless, temperamental and utterly selfish.'

'She does need you though – even though you don't actually live with her.'

'No,' he said. 'Not now. She got over the accident well. She's learned to adapt. She can get around by herself. She has a motorised wheelchair as well as a folding one, and a car. She can feed herself, shower, dress herself. I do nothing for her any more.'

'You're there for her though. You have to be there for her.'

'What as, for goodness sake? Her pet dog?' His tone was bitter.

Cass swallowed. 'These things happen. We have to make sacrifices.'

'Yes.' He slid down from the wall. 'I suppose so. But this conversation is pointless. We'd better get back down to the market square. Trent wants me to check the bike tyres for this afternoon's session on the moor.' He stood directly in front of her. 'We can't have anything going wrong for Trent's pet protégé – your friend Teasdale, can we?'

'Dillon doesn't want to be singled out. He's just enjoying doing this.'

'Trent's quite taken with him. Says he could probably

groom him for stardom.' He gave a twisted little smile. 'If you don't want that for him, you'd better warn the lad.'

'Dillon's twenty-four – hardly a "lad" who doesn't know what he's doing,' she retorted. 'And I doubt he'd take advice from me, or from anybody else for that matter – I'm not exactly a mother figure, am I? Especially not to somebody as old as Dillon.'

'You're twenty-seven, Cass. Wake up! He's not for you. He isn't a man, he's merely playing at life. At the moment I think he'd rather marry a Harley than a girl.'

'I think so too.' A smile formed round her mouth.

'And that doesn't worry you?' He seemed perplexed.

She shook her head. 'I'm not looking for a husband, Patric. When I met Dillon, I was looking for an electrician, okay?'

'A pity – about the husband bit.'

'Why?'

'You could have me. Any time. You know that though, don't you?'

'And Michelle?'

'Michelle can go to hell. It's where she belongs.' He swung away from her and she ran after him, fell into step with him as they went down the hill to the market square.

'Stop thinking just about yourself,' she said in a light voice. 'Stop playing the martyr – it doesn't suit you.'

He glanced at her. 'You thought about yourself, when you walked out on me. I'd say it was exactly the same thing – you were thinking of yourself, Cass – you never stopped to wonder what might happen to me when you left Suffolk.'

Keeping her temper in check, she said, 'I didn't walk out on you. There was nothing left for us after Michelle had that accident. You known darn well there wasn't. We couldn't have carried on seeing each other after that.'

He stopped and turned to her, shooting out a hand and halting her in her tracks. His fingers were warm and hard on her arm. 'You thought that *then* – when Michelle was helpless, but what about now?'

'Now?' She stared at him.

'We could start to build on what we once had. Michelle's a survivor – she'll find some other poor sod to run rings around her before much longer.'

'Do I have to wait until then?' she asked. 'Do I have to get Michelle's gracious permission to take up my life again – with you?'

'Cass…' He looked deeply into her eyes. 'I never stopped loving you.'

'But things are different now.'

'No,' he said. 'We're still the same two people we always were.'

'Except…' She stopped what she was saying, realising she'd been about to blurt out the truth – tell him about Tiffany.

'Except what, Cass?' He reached out both hands and grasped hold of hers. 'Except what? Tell me.'

His fingers tightened around hers. It was like the old days. She felt warm and loved and protected again. But *she* was the protector now, she realised. And she had to protect Tiff at all costs. She couldn't have the baby drawn into this sorry affair, couldn't risk Patric wanting access to the baby – taking her away each weekend like lots of fathers did nowadays – taking her to his Suffolk home – and maybe running the risk of Michelle coming into contact with Tiff.

She shook herself mentally.

'What are you trying to say?' he insisted.

A voice yelled from close behind them. 'What the hell are you two doing? Do I have to tell ya ten thousand times that we've gotta get up on them there moors and set things in motion?'

She gasped out, 'Trent!' and dragged her hands away from Patric's.

'Damn the man.' Patric swung round.

Trent was jogging up from the square towards them. He looked cool and unflustered in a bright yellow shirt and camel shorts that showed off his magnificent tan. He stood still, ten yards away from them both and jabbed a finger at them.

'Twelve-twenty, I said. Twelve fu… Aw, hell, Sandie-baby, I can't get outa' the habit of giving way to my feelings.' He glanced at Patric, then pointedly at his watch. 'It is now twelve-thirty-two and twenty-one seconds, and we oughta all be on board the trucks and heading up there.' The jabbing finger stabbed the air in the direction of the high moorland. 'Get it? This is a job we're on. Right? Time costs dollars! So get to it, OK?'

Cass couldn't keep a straight face. She burst out laughing. 'OK,' she said. 'You're the boss – *Mister* Trent.'

'Glad you've realised that fact – at last, *Mizz Sandie*,' he said, following it up with, 'Yes, sir-ee – I'm the boss of this here outfit, and it's now…' he looked down at his watch again, 'it is now twelve-thirty-four and…'

'OK!' Patric held up one hand, then laughingly added, 'So dock my wages, Aaron. See if I care!'

And Cass felt glad that at least Patric hadn't entirely lost his sense of humour, and could still see the funny side of things.

chapter nine

Michelle Faulkner had parked her car some distance away from where they were filming. The moorland roads around here were good, she found, and it didn't give her a lot of discomfort, walking from the car to the point where a small spread-out crowd had gathered to watch what was happening.

The scene they were doing had called for motorbikes to bump and swerve over the rough-tufted humps of heather and coarse grass and there had been quite a few casualties and bruised egos in the past hour. The scene had been filmed time-and-time again, but not once had every biker managed to stay seated till the end.

The man in the yellow shirt was shouting for order again. 'One last time,' Michelle heard him yell. 'One time. That's all I ask for. But if any one of you blockheads comes off this time – I'm warning you – I'm sending out for a bath of super-glue, and I'll stick you clowns down by the seat of your pants if necessary. Are you hearing me?'

Michelle choked back her laughter as the onlookers cheered. Trent was someone to be reckoned with, she decided. He looked like one of the tough-and-no-nonsense guys – nothing artificial about him. 'What you see is what you get,' she muttered to herself. 'And boy – is he sexy?'

One of the gang yelled back, 'Man – get on this bike and let's see if an oldie like you can do any better than the professionals in this game, huh?'

'Aw, kid, I could leave you standin',' came the shout. 'I

was riding them things when you were a toothless wonder in kindergarten.'

Michelle threw back her head, roaring with laughter and, although she was at least a hundred yards away, the light breeze must have carried the sound farther than she'd anticipated it would.

Yellow shirt swung round towards her and promptly strode out in her direction.

He stood on the other side of the barrier that kept the onlookers away from the set, and faced her squarely. 'You find something funny, Mam?'

Close up, she saw he was older than she'd imagined him to be – in his early fifties, she reckoned, but he wore his years well and the creases in his face were those put there by laughter and good living.

'I assume you're the great Aaron Trent,' she said.

'You assume correct!' he snapped.

Just then she saw Patric coming up at a run behind him, so she put on her brightest smile for Trent and leaned heavily on the crutches that supported her these days.

'You should have a seat…' Trent began, but Patric with a face like fury skidded to a halt beside him and ended whatever it was Trent was about to say by giving vent to his own feelings.

'Michelle – what the hell are you doing here?'

Before she could answer, Aaron Trent spun round on Patric. 'I take it this is your lady wife?'

'My *ex*-wife!' Patric aimed his next words at her. 'Why didn't you tell me you were going to spring something like this?'

Trent butted in. 'Hey – that's no way to talk to a lady.'

Michelle thought the time had come for her to say something. 'I was bored. It seemed like a good idea at the time.'

She shrugged. 'I'm quite enjoying it.'

'Then come and enjoy it this side of the fence,' Trent said amiably.

She put on a pretty act. 'I can't, Mr Trent. I left my car way back there.' She half-turned away from him, indicating with a jut of her chin where the car was parked.

'Patric, old man, go get that car and take it down into that there village.' Trent beamed at her and moving aside one of the barriers in front of her said, 'Allow me to be the perfect gentleman, Mrs Faulkner, and invite you to join us.'

Michelle eased through the barrier, a little awkwardly on the crutches, and Aaron Trent put out a hand to steady her. Patric, his face impassive now, but his eyes showing his disapproval of her, shot out a hand and said, 'Keys, Michelle. I need your car keys if I'm to shift the damn thing.'

She paused, pushed a hand into the pocket of her bright blue three-quarter-length padded coat and pulled out the keys which she dropped into his hand. As Trent moved to put the barrier back in place, Patric said in a low voice to her, 'I see you've deserted your usual mourning black, Michelle – blue coat, grey pants and sea-green sweater. What's it all in aid of, I wonder?'

'I want to take an interest in your work, darling.' She spoke softly and smiled sweetly at him. 'I also think the time for mourning Craig Andrews – and my own crippling infirmity – is over.'

Patric stared at her for perhaps half-a-minute or so, obviously trying to make sense of her words, but Trent was dancing attention on her again now so he went off towards the car.

Trent led her the best way he could over the tussocky grass and Michelle found it hard going but didn't complain. He dragged a fold-away chair out for her when they reached one of the vans and it was with relief that she sank down onto it.

'Patric should have told me you wanted to come,' Trent said, his brow furrowed. 'I'd have sent a car for you. You look like you're in some pain, Mrs Faulkner.'

'I'm OK. Really.' She fought down the pain in her legs and meeting his glance boldly said, 'Please call me Michelle.'

He grinned. 'Call me Trent,' he replied. 'They all do around here. I sometimes forget I have a first name so I don't usually answer to it.'

'Maybe I'll think up my own name for you.' She knew she was flirting with him but she didn't care. He was an attractive man showing her some interest and the interest was mutual. Those shorts – they showed off his legs to advantage. He kept himself in trim. They weren't the kind of legs usually associated with a fifty-year-old. She was interested in the man – very interested, she decided.

'Your own name, eh. That would be interesting – Michelle.'

She had him hooked. His eyes were lazy as they roamed over her from top to toe. Some men shied away from the crutches, she knew. Others though, the bolder ones, they saw things the others didn't. A well-kept body, for instance, slim as a teenager, firm as an athlete, with supple skin, heavy lidded dark eyes and swept-back, loosely-coiled ebony hair.. She could put on a subtle charm as well – when she wanted something. And she wanted Aaron Trent. She'd known that within minutes of meeting him.

Motorbikes were revving all around her. Arc lights were set up and Patric had clearly been right about the trailing wires, camera crews, and the general air of mayhem that accompanied the filming.

Trent had moved away now and was shouting orders. 'One more time – and make it good.' He tilted his head back and looked to where dark clouds were forming overhead. 'And I mean – *make it good*,' he repeated in a louder voice. 'We're in for a storm – and that's the last thing we need.'

Michelle watched it all with interest. One of the bikers was good – the lead one. What he looked like she had no idea, since he was clad in black leather and the helmet he wore was all concealing. He wheeled and dodged the roughest ground, doing delicate balancing acts most of the time to avoid being thrown from the machine. He was an excellent rider though – and didn't he just know it! He banked over in all the right places, cornered at constant speeds that avoided the necessity for braking and obsolete gear changes. He positioned himself correctly for every turn like a graceful dancer, crossing the path of other bikes, effortlessly overtaking, then swinging back into convoy.

Michelle felt a gathering excitement inside her. This was how life should be working out for her, she felt. Life should be fast and dangerous at times. It was a long time since she'd felt like this – young and fit, and ready for anything. Adrenaline pulsed through her veins as she watched first the bikers and then Aaron Trent. On the job, he was giving it everything he'd got. He was part and parcel of the screaming bikes, the lights, the tense atmosphere and the absolute magical precision of those bikers.

She was sorry when the show ended and the arc lights dimmed to nothing. The afternoon was cloudy and dark again. Some of the magic disappeared – but Aaron Trent was still there and Patric hadn't returned from taking her car down to the village. She wondered if Cass Fairburn was around somewhere – maybe in one of the motor vans? Or perhaps Cass had stayed down in the village, and Patric was with her right now?

'Some show, huh?'

Trent was at her side again, happy that the scene had gone well, and attentive as ever. He told her he'd take her down to the village in his car – and she could pick her own up there if she wanted to.

'Is there an alternative?' she asked archly.

'To what, Michelle?' He was playing her at her own game.

'To me picking my car up, of course.'

'You could always let me take you for a meal?'

'In your car?'

'That's right, Ma'am.' He made a slight, mocking bow.

'Is it a big one? Your car?'

'A limo. Pure white. Pure joy.'

'I'd be happy to accompany you then…Trent.'

'You haven't found a pet name for me yet, then…Michelle?' His eyes were crinkling at the corners. He looked like a man enjoying himself.

'Still thinking about it, Trent.'

Filming had finished for the day.

She loved his limo.

On the way back, he said he'd have to go back to his hotel first to change for dinner.

She said she'd go with him and wait.

It all worked out exactly as she wanted it.

They dined in his room. And Michelle didn't return home that night.

She left a message on the bungalow's answer-phone for Patric some time later, while Trent took a shower.

'Don't worry about me, darling! I'm being well taken care of! I'll see you sometime tomorrow!'

chapter ten

'Cass – I was wondering…?' Greer Stuart paused as she sat at the kitchen table of the flat feeding Tiffany her mashed-up breakfast cereal, 'Would you mind if I brought Tiffany over to Ashton today to watch the film being made? The local newspaper's been full of it, with photos and things, and I'd love the chance to come and see what's happening.'

Cass wasn't deliriously enthusiastic at the idea of Tiffany and Patric being in the same place at the same time. But Greer had been dropping hints all week, and now that she had come straight out and asked, Cass knew it would be unkind of her to deny the girl an opportunity to see what almost the whole of Derbyshire had been watching for the past month or so.

'Well…' she began.

'We'd keep well away from the actual filming. We wouldn't get in the way.'

Cass checked her bag to give herself time to think. She liked to make sure that she had her phone, the script of the film, and all the other usual bits and pieces she carried around with her.

'They don't let you get anywhere near the cameras.' She looked up and smiled warmly, seeing the eagerness in Greer's face. 'There are barriers to keep onlookers well back from the action.'

'Yes. I know.' A note of excitement crept into Greer's voice. 'I saw it on TV. They were interviewing that man on the local news programme the other night – the one who's in charge of things. He's a real dish, isn't he?'

'Aaron Trent?' Cass looked up. 'He's drumming up all the publicity he can get at the moment. I thought it was a good interview he gave.'

'Do you really mind if we come?' Greer looked worriedly at her employer. 'I mean – it won't do Tiffany any harm, will it?'

Dryly, Cass said, 'Not unless she bumps into her daddy.' She sighed and stared across the table at Greer. 'If you *do* come, you will be careful, won't you? I wouldn't want Patric Faulkner coming within a hundred yards of her.'

'But he doesn't know she exists, does he? It's not as if he'll be looking for her, is it? There must be other people with kiddies there, so if he sees a girl with a baby in a buggy, there's no chance he's going to take any notice of her, is there?'

Put like that, Cass supposed Greer had a point. She chewed worriedly on her lip however. She'd heard how Michelle Faulkner had got herself noticed by Trent a couple of days ago – how he'd moved the barriers back for her, given her a seat, and had then disappeared – after filming was completed – with Michelle tucked up neatly in his car. She hadn't been there herself. She'd left early – and was glad now that she'd had an appointment to take Tiff for one of her baby-immunisations that day.

'You don't actually *know* Patric personally though. I'm just worried in case he sees Tiff accidentally and starts asking questions.'

Greer's eager eyes misted over. 'Oh, heck. I never thought of that.'

Looking at the problem logically, Cass knew that the chance of Patric actually meeting Greer head-on was virtually a thousand-to-one. Patric *never* went beyond the barriers that kept the fans and onlookers away from the set. And even if he glimpsed a girl and a baby among the crowd, he would be too far away to see the resemblance Tiffany bore to himself.

'Hang on,' she said. 'I've got a photo of him. If I show you that…'

Returning from her bedroom with the photograph, Cass handed it to Greer. 'Take a good look – and remember him,' she said with a grin.

'Wow! He's okay, isn't he? I won't forget him in a hurry.' Greer handed the picture back. 'I'll keep right away from anyone tall, dark and handsome – just in case he's changed since having that photo taken.'

'He hasn't,' Cass said, picking up her bag, dropping a kiss on Tiff's head and walking over to the door. 'Tell you what – I'll look out for you there later in the morning and we can maybe go and have a pub lunch in the next village. Well away from Ashton and the filming.'

Greer spooned the last of Tiff's mashed-up cereal into the little girl's mouth and looking up, her face wreathed in smiles. 'That'll be nice. You don't mind though, do you? About us coming to Ashton? It'll be so exciting.'

The good weather was here now, but Cass recalled thinking it had been anything *but* exciting when she'd been standing ankle deep in mud in a cold Ashton dawn for the scenes where the river had broken its banks and had flooded several fields just over a week ago.

She said as much to Greer, but the girl only laughed and turned away, telling the baby in a loud whisper, 'We're going to see Mummy at work today.'

In the bungalow that Patric and Michelle were sharing on the moors, Michelle Faulkner was up early and making coffee in the spacious kitchen.

She heard Patric's footsteps in the passage and turned awkwardly to face the door as he entered the room.

'What are you doing up at this hour? Are you okay?' He stood, clad only in a dark-coloured, tightly-belted bathrobe, his hair still wet from his early morning shower.

'I couldn't sleep – and there's no law prohibiting me getting up at six-thirty and making my "husband's" breakfast, is there?'

'Breakfast! Michelle, you know I don't eat much at this time of day. And I am not your husband.'

'Lightly-scrambled eggs and toast won't hurt, will it?' she asked pleasantly, ignoring his last comment.

'As you've made it, I might as well eat it.' He moved over to the table, pulled a chair out from under it and sat down.

She was wearing a white bathrobe that enveloped her from the chin down to her ankles. She spun a heated food trolley round towards the table and said, 'Here – help yourself while I pour the coffee. I'm getting quite domesticated.'

'Shall I put some breakfast out for you too?' His voice, she noted, was strained and she wondered when he'd get round to asking her about that night she'd spent away from the bungalow. Deliberately, she hadn't brought the subject up.

She shook her head. 'I've had mine, thanks.'

'Michelle…' he paused for a second as he helped himself from the trolley. 'Michelle – are you up to something?'

She turned round to face him, a delicate china cup and saucer balancing in her hand as she steadied herself with just one of her crutches. 'What *do* you mean?' she asked in a lilting, but mocking, voice.

'Well,' he spread his hands, indicating the breakfast, the coffee and her. 'We don't usually do this sort of thing, do we? I can't remember the last time I even *saw* you at this time in the morning. And,' he added cautiously, 'There was that night you didn't come back here. Your life's your own, of course, but…'

She laughed, amused at his careful words. Ignoring his last statement though, she said, 'You *could* see me any time of the day you like, Patric. It was your decision – not mine – for us to have separate bedrooms up here in Derbyshire, remember?'

She leant over to the table, placed the cup of coffee beside his plate.

He glanced up at her. 'It was a mutual thing. Our marriage is over. We haven't shared a bedroom for almost five years. What point is there in kidding yourself that the relationship can be salvaged?'

'It doesn't have to be like that. We're both of us different people. I've lost Craig and you've lost your Cass. Perhaps it was meant to be like this – so we could stand back and take a good, long look at what we once had.'

He was remote from her. Instinctively, she knew it would take more than one lousy breakfast and a lavish dowsing of Chanel to woo him back into her arms.

He said in a hard voice, 'The divorce was the final and proper end to our marriage.'

'We still see each other every day though.' She was very near him, she reached out a soft, manicured hand and laid it gently on his arm.

She felt the muscles of his wrist stiffen as he turned his head towards her and said, 'And you know why that is, don't you? You hated it in that nursing home – made life such hell for the staff that they refused to have you there.

So, somebody had to take responsibility for you...'

Her hand fell away from him. She took a step back and wouldn't meet his gaze until she'd moved even further away and the table was between them.

'I don't want your pity – or your blame. And I think I'm proving to you and to anyone else who cares to see, that I can manage most things by myself now.' The words were scornful. She'd rehearsed them well. 'I want what we once had – what we both valued. A good marriage. A partnership. We could make it work again, I know we could.'

He carried on eating his breakfast and several minutes elapsed before he said, 'There's nothing I can give you, *except* pity, Michelle.'

For a moment, she knew panic. She'd been so sure of her power over him. Her mind worked swiftly. 'I'm not asking for it all at once. I know that love has to be given time...'

'Love!' He laughed then, softly but with a bitterness that struck at her heart. 'Love?' His voice was incredulous. 'Surely you don't think there's any of that still lurking around in this particular relationship, do you?'

'You loved me once.' Her chin came up in a defiant gesture.

'Yes, I did,' he admitted. 'But love can only take so much before it dies.'

Her hand clenched furiously on the metal crutch she depended upon; she had difficulty keeping her temper in check and not flinging something at him. For preference, it would have been the pot of scalding coffee she'd made for them both, but she fought down the urge and realised that nothing would be achieved by her losing her temper. She'd done that too often in the past. He was well used to it – to tantrums and shouting and arguments. It wasn't all those things that had killed their love though – it had been her own stupidity, her own selfish lust for a man who'd been years younger than herself. A kid really when measured at the side of Patric. But Craig had been a flatterer, and a born seducer.

And it hadn't bothered her then that she'd hurt Patric, that she'd practically thrown him into the arms of Cass Fairburn. She couldn't let it bother her now either, she decided. There was too much at stake.

'It wasn't all my fault. Craig and I – we worked together, you knew that. Of necessity we were thrown together. I tried not to be attracted to him, but you were spending so much time at that damned motor-racing circuit in Cambridge, you didn't seem to care what I was doing.'

Patric had finished his breakfast, he pushed his chair back and stood up. 'Don't tell me he took advantage of you,' he said. 'Because I won't believe it, Michelle.'

'You know how these things start up…'

'Yes,' he said, 'they start up when one married partner no longer has any use for the other one.'

He walked towards the door. She moved a little bit too fast and lost her balance, collapsing in a heap at his feet with the crutch wrenched from her hand by the fall.

He was beside her in seconds, helping her up, handing over the crutch again, asking, 'Are you OK?' But there was no real caring in his tone, she noted.

She was shaken, but not hurt. She told him so.

'Sit down and have a drink.'

'Make one for me, darling.' She glanced up at him. 'Please?'

He looked at his watch. Sighed. Then he went over to the trolley and poured her a coffee. By that time she'd worked her way across the kitchen and was sitting at the table in the chair he'd vacated.

He put the drink down in front of her. 'Do you want your pills? Have you hurt your legs?'

She put a hand on his. 'I'm OK, Patric. But I do want something.'

'Well, tell me…'

She saw him looking round the kitchen.

'Not anything like that.'

She felt a tenseness in the air as he turned back to her.

'Oh? What is it you want then?'

'I want a baby, Patric.'

He just stared at her. Then he laughed and the sound was harsh. 'Jokes aren't my cup of tea at this time in the morning,' he said.

'I'm not joking. I have never been so serious in my life before. I mean it, Patric. I want a baby before it's too late. After all, I'm nearing forty.'

'Is that where you were – that night? Talking babies? With Trent?'

'I was in a hotel room.' She looked away from him before adding, 'Alone, Patric.'

'You left the film set with Aaron Trent,' he accused.

'I stayed at Aaron Trent's hotel,' she replied tautly. 'I told you though – I was alone.' The lie came easier with each telling of it. 'I needed to think. I needed to get away from this damned bungalow where you and I are always getting in one another's way and where we do nothing but fight, and air our differences.'

He turned away from her, but hot anger suddenly surged through her and she shouted, 'Come back. We have to talk. You always walk away from me when I want to *talk*.'

'There's nothing left to say.' He pushed his hands into the pockets of his bathrobe and waited for her to move.

She stayed put. 'You had an affair too.' Her head jerked

up. You can't say I was entirely to blame. You soon found consolation when our marriage hit the rocks. And Cass Fairburn can take a share of the blame for that.'

'Mine was hardly an "affair",' he said. 'Nothing happened between Cass and me until after the divorce came through.'

'I suppose you're going to say that was *my* fault? That I threw you into her arms?'

'No,' he said. 'It wasn't planned though – Cass and me. I didn't deliberately go out looking for a bed mate.'

Her laugh was brittle. 'It just happened, I suppose. I could throw the old saying at you that 'accidents never *happen* – they are always *caused*.' Does the same hold good for *affairs* – I wonder?'

'Yes. I'd say it was something like that. Cass and I were old friends. I'd known her for years, remember? She was always someone I could trust, so maybe I did make the affair *happen*. Whatever it was though, Michelle, we were happy, Cass and I, and you were out of my life by then.'

'And now?'

'It's over between you and me. You know it is.' The words were explosive.

'Are you sure?' She watched him closely as she half-turned in her seat with one arm draped over its back.

'Perfectly sure.' His face was impassive.

'Make love to me – and then tell me you *don't* love me,' she challenged.

He gave a frozen laugh of disbelief, then followed it up with, 'Why should I? I don't even find you attractive now. It would be obscene.'

'You didn't always feel like this.'

'No,' he agreed, 'I must have been blind not to see through you in the past. I did love you once, but I don't feel anything for you now.' He was blunt and to the point and all kindness was put aside. 'This is the end, Michelle. Why can't you just accept that?'

'Lots of men think they've fallen out of love with their wives. I don't suppose prostitutes care anything for the men they have sex with. But you could give me a child. A baby of my own,' she argued.

'And why should I do that?' He moved further away from her, towards the door. 'Do you really think I want to tie myself down to you any more than I'm already shackled?'

'I'd see you were suitably repaid.'

'Repaid, Michelle? What are you saying?' He had stopped now, had swung round to look at her. She could almost feel sorry for him, but wouldn't let herself do that.

'I'm talking about a proposition,' she said. 'Give me a baby – and you can be rid of me and marry your precious Cass.'

'What!' He stared at her incredulously.

'I mean it,' she said. 'I accept that we have nothing in common anymore. I accept that you don't love me. But I need someone – I want a baby. Give me that, and you can go. I'll sign any agreement you want me to. But I need you to give me that child.'

She saw him shaking his head, as if it were full of something he didn't like and was trying to get rid of it. It didn't do her morale much good, knowing how the thought of making love to her was so repulsive to him. She required his co-operation however for that one last thing he could do for her.

When he spoke, it was softly, and with venom. 'I'm not some bloody "stud", Michelle. And this is one thing I can't put on an act for.' He stood straight and tall in front of her and again he shook his head. 'It's impossible. I just don't feel anything like that for you now. If you want a kid – you'll just have to find yourself somebody else to provide the service, but I wouldn't advise motherhood – not for you. It's just another excuse to have power over somebody, and a helpless child would suit you just fine, wouldn't it?'

He was gone, turning on his heel and slamming out of the room, leaving her trembling and shaken. And then the tears came – of anger and frustration and the knowledge that she would never, ever, get him back. There was still Aaron Trent however. And Aaron had no qualms about making love to her – he'd proved that several times over on the night she'd spent with him. Heat flooded her face as she remembered that night, and she realised she could well be pregnant even now by Trent. But it was Patric she wanted, and there had to be a way of getting him back. But how was she going to do that?

chapter eleven

Cass sat inside the motorhome. Opposite her was Patric, and walking up and down was Aaron Trent. A problem had arisen.

'You two have got to get your heads together and fix things,' Trent stated, halting his restless pacing to hold out both hands towards them in a gesture of finality. 'I want the bike in the river, see? And this guy…'

'The rider?' Patric broke in.

'Yeah! That's right. I want him right there with it – face down. Dead. Or looking as much like dead as possible. OK?'

'The river's especially deep at that spot,' Cass said, worried. 'Can't you do a mock-up? A tank full of water or something? Or even film the scene at a place where the current isn't quite so dangerous?'

'Nope!' Trent would make no compromise. 'Sandie-baby, you know where it has to be. You wrote it into the screenplay – remember?'

Icily she said, 'I obviously didn't realise that it would mean putting somebody's life in danger – just for the sake of your TV drama.'

Inside she was fuming. She hadn't reckoned on Trent making changes to her original screenplay, and she didn't like it. There had been many times just lately, when she just wanted to throw in her hand and tell him to get on with it any way he chose – but to leave her out of it.

'Cass *is* right.' Patric spoke again. 'It's too dangerous.

Any fool can see that, Aaron. It's absolute madness putting lives at risk, – the rider as well as the camera crew – who'll need a mock-up raft of some sort, for that matter.'

'I am not a fool!' Trent was digging his heels in to a degree that Cass had not believed possible. 'Look,' he went on in an irate voice, 'This is a high spot of the damn film. It's got to be authentic. It's got to be right. And that weir across the river *is* the right spot. We're making an action drama! Do I have to remind you of that?'

'You're making it into a full-scale disaster drama,' Cass said, tight-lipped.

Patric added the weight of his argument too. 'It's like a whirlpool beyond the weir. You know that, Trent.'

'We're insured, dammit. I can cover any poxy claim that comes up.'

'Even if somebody gets killed?'

Trent pointed an accusing finger at Patric. 'You are getting too melodramatic,' he yelled. 'Everybody knows the risks and, if they choose to take them, then I can't see what you're making such a helluva fuss about.'

'It's too dangerous,' Cass cried, thumping the table with a clenched fist in agitation, and knowing what she said was true. 'Trent, see sense, will you? There are all those people out there – watching what we do. They're local folk and they know this stretch of river. They're just waiting for you to make a slip and I for one, won't stand for it!'

'Cass is right.' Patric broke in.

'No, she ain't. And don't keep calling her 'Cass'. She's "Sandie" – while she's working for me. She's *Sandie* – got it?'

'You take this damn play-acting too far,' Patric said, glaring at Cass as he addressed Trent. 'Why don't you tell him?' he threw at her. 'Why don't you just tell him you want to be yourself? Why do you let him walk all over you, Cass?'

'I don't let anybody walk all over me,' she seethed.

'Yes you do. Even to the point of losing your identity.'

She leaned back in her seat; she was growing increasingly weary of all this hassle. 'We're getting off the point,' she said, hanging on to her temper with difficulty. '*I'm* not the problem. The stunt-man is. Why don't you bring him in here and let us put the risks to him? Why are you keeping us in the dark as to who he is?'

'It doesn't matter who he is,' Trent ranted. 'Hell, woman, are you the director here, or am I?'

Quietly, Patric said, 'You've got to make it clear to him, Aaron. I won't go along with this bike stunt if the fellow's not in full possession of the facts.'

Trent threw his hands up in the air. 'OK! I'll send him in. He knows what he's up against though. He knows the damn river better than I do. It's the Harley guy. The "leader of the gang", and he's…'

'Dillon!' Cass leapt to her feet, her heart pounding. 'Dillon Teasdale? What on earth are you thinking of, Trent? You can't use Dillon – he's not a stunt-man! He's just an electrician who happens to be mad about bikes. He's only an average swimmer and with all that leather gear on, he won't stand a chance of coming out of that river alive.'

'We can fix the gear so it peels off easily.' Trent sank down into a chair and rubbed a hand across his forehead. 'Hell, Sandie-baby, I'm not that stupid. Wardrobe's taking the measurements now. There'll be strips of that sticky-zipper stuff holding it together. I tell you – it peels off – it peels off like a fu… – like skin off an orange.' He shot out a hand to her, 'Go and see if you don't believe me. And he won't be wearing actual bikers leathers. What he'll be wearing is a thin satiny stuff that looks like leather. You don't really think I'd toss the guy in the river weighed down with a ton of *real* bike gear, do you?'

Sarcastically Patric said, 'How *dare* we think such a thing. So – you're going to have him riding over that rough ground first of all in a satin jump suit – where if he has a fall, he'll have no protection whatsoever in the way of clothing…'

'Do me a favour!' Trent gazed vacantly up at the ceiling, then back at Patric. 'Haven't you learned nothin' while you've been here? The Teasdale guy will be in proper leathers while he's riding the bike – OK? He'll have the best protection we can offer, like the European Certificate stuff he's riding around in right now: Kevlar panels, armour in all the right places and a carbon fibre helmet that's as tough as the helm of my "Ocean Lady" yacht. Anyhow, back to the damn river scene. We "cut" just as he reaches the river-bank. He gets off the bike, changes into the satin and, if you like I'll knit him a woolly vest to put on under-neath it so the poor jerk doesn't catch cold.' He smiled a grim smile of sarcasm, then went on, 'Then, we swap the bike.'

'You do what?' Cass sat down and leaned forward over the table, her shoulders hunched. She wanted to be sure that Dillon would come to no harm, and she realised that Trent knew his job, but…

Trent was explaining now. 'We swap the bike for a wreck that's been doctored to look like the Harley. You surely don't think I'm going to send thirty-thousand dollars worth of pure Milwaukee metal into the damn river, do you? It's not something I can replace. That Harley is a genuine limited edition.'

In a calm but decisive voice, Cass said, 'Dillon Teasdale's a limited edition too. A one-off, you could say. He can't be replaced either.'

Patric Faulkner shot her a glance of sheer venom. 'No,' he said, 'I'll bet he can't. Not in your estimation anyway.'

Trent made for the door. 'Look – if you two are going to get personal, you can fight it out between yourselves,' he said. 'If you want to consult Teasdale – consult away. He won't change his mind though.'

When he'd gone with a slamming of the motorhome door, Cass said, 'How can he say that?'

'He's paying your darling Dillon way over the odds,' Patric said. 'Didn't you know that? He's even offered him a screen-test. He's dangling the golden carrot in front of him to get him to play ball. Teasdale's impressionable. If Trent says jump – he'll jump.'

'No! Dillon's not stupid.' She shook her head.

'He didn't tell you?' Patric faced her across the table. 'Lover-boy Teasdale didn't tell you about the screen-test?'

Cass stood up, planted both hands squarely on the table in front of her and leaned over it till her face was only inches away from Patric Faulkner. She looked straight into his eyes. 'There's nothing – absolutely *nothing* between Dillon and me, except a perfectly harmless friendship,' she said in a furious voice.

Before she knew what he was doing, his hand shot out and grasped her jaw, and he half-rose out of his seat. Then his mouth was crushing down on her lips, forcing them apart, and reminding her all over again of what it had been like when they'd been lovers.

In that instant, it was second nature to respond to him – eagerly, passionately as her lips parted, clinging to his. She closed her eyes and allowed herself to remember a time that had been pushed into the farthest recesses of her mind – a time so long ago. More than a year had passed but she recalled it in detail. How could she ever forget it; in her mind, in her heart, she knew that baby Tiffany had been conceived then, conceived out of a love that Cass knew, for her, would exist until eternity.

The cottage in Suffolk had been a refuge for them both that raw February night, and their need of each other had been urgent. She remembered it as if it was yesterday…

'I was scared you wouldn't be able to get away from Michelle…'

Lying in her old-fashioned bed, he hushed her with one finger against her lips as she leaned over him. 'Don't mention her name, Cass – not here. Here belongs to you and me. Here is where nobody can intrude. Here is where I want to be – always, and I will be soon. Everything's settled. I've got my own place and Michelle is staying at "Lilacs" – her old family home. It's all plain-sailing. I'm a free man, sweetheart.'

'I can't believe it's really happening – can't convince myself that she won't try one last time to stir up trouble.'

He pulled her down to him and kissed her. It was a warm, golden kiss – golden because of the light from the low lamp on the oak ottoman, golden because it was a good and solid and richly-rewarding love she felt for him. His lips were still touching hers as he said, 'She's got Craig Andrews now, Cass. She's made a new life of her own. Things are falling into place for us, my darling. We'll be married before summer comes – you and I. I really believe that nothing can come between us now…'

It had been tempting fate – saying something like that. Cass knew that now, as gently she eased away from him and regained, at least, a small measure of composure again.

'You still care!' His voice was soft. 'Cass – we have to

make plans…'

She came back with a jolt to the present day and, almost angrily, she pulled away from him, swung round towards the door of the motorhome. His voice followed her. 'Cass – don't go. We have to talk, there's such a lot to catch up on.'

She pulled the door open and threw back at him, 'That should never have happened, and there's nothing to talk about – you had no right…'

'No right to what?' The voice was cool and amused. A woman's voice. Right behind her.

She whirled at the sound, and found herself staring down into a face she had never wanted to see again in the whole of her life.

Michelle Faulkner was her usual immaculate, confident self. And even though she was holding firmly onto her crutches, she was still regal, still beautiful as ever.

'Cass Fairburn! Well! Well! Well! Do you know – I had an idea I might find you two together.' She leaned sideways a little to peer through the door beyond Cass. 'Ah, yes. My darling, caring Patric. It becomes clearer by the minute now – why you didn't want *me* to come to Derbyshire with you.'

Patric moved to her side now, and Cass heard the impatience in his voice as he spoke to the woman waiting to enter the motorhome. 'What do you want, Michelle? Why are you here?'

'I was bored.' Michelle glanced meaningfully at Cass. 'Not that you'd know the meaning of the word, I suppose. You seem to have plenty with which to occupy yourself!'

Cass looked at Patric. 'I can't stay, Patric.' She realised she was chickening out of a difficult situation, but she didn't want a scene and, feeling as she did right now, she knew that tears weren't far away. Her life was getting all messed up again. History was repeating itself because they'd met up again – in different surroundings, in different circumstances, but the feelings they'd once shared were still the same. He still loved her, she knew. And it was the same with her. Ever since they'd met up again, she'd known, deep down inside her, that it would only be a matter of time before…

She shook herself and tried to rid her mind of all emotion. She had to look at this thing clearly and logically. It was Michelle who needed him – Michelle who had a claim on him even though they were no longer married. It should be so simple, she realised, but it wasn't. While Michelle was on the scene, Patric would never be free.

Fear played a part in her reasoning too, for she had no doubt at all in her mind that it had been Michelle who'd scared Greer on the riverside a week or two ago. She stared at the woman now, and a tight knot of despair curled in the pit of her stomach. What kind of woman was Michelle? To what ends would she go in order to keep Patric with her? A man she had never loved and who didn't love her.

Blindly, Cass turned away and ran down the steps of the motorhome, leaving Patric with the wife who had betrayed him – but who still seemed to have such a tight hold over him.

chapter twelve

It wasn't easy to get rid of Michelle. She was intent of seeing Aaron Trent, and it was only when Patric managed to convince her that Trent had gone across several fields and down to the river to finalise plans for the controversial scene they'd been discussing, that she got in her car and drove off.

Cass, too, had gone, Patric noted. Her car was nowhere to be seen. It was nearing lunchtime; there had been no rolling of cameras that day because Trent had got a bee in his bonnet about the river scene – and Patric knew he wouldn't rest until he'd convinced everybody it was perfectly safe to go ahead.

Trent was adamant that the river scene should get underway as soon as possible, and for two pins, Patric felt as though he'd like to walk out on the lot of them and leave them to it.

There was only one thing stopping him returning to Suffolk however – and that was his resolve to win Cass over again, and see that she didn't mess up her life by falling for Dillon Teasdale – which, as far as he was concerned, seemed a distinct possibility.

He turned just once as he reached the door of the 'Lead Miner' pub where he was going for a bite of lunch, and way across the valley, beyond the market square, he caught a glimpse of a blonde head against some trees on the opposite hillside, beyond the barriers that kept the local onlookers away from where filming would be taking place.

'Teasdale!' he muttered. 'I wonder if it's *her* he's talking to.

But it wasn't Cass, he saw, as he strained his eyes against the sunlight. The biker was talking to a girl, but it certainly wasn't Cass. This girl had red-gold hair – nothing like Cass's. He felt sure he'd seen her somewhere before and he struggled to think where.

Then it hit him. She'd been there the day he'd bumped into Cass in Rydale Tor. She'd been sitting on a bench beside the river – and she'd had a baby with her in a buggy.

He stood still and watched, drawing in his breath as she bent down now to the buggy-thing against her legs and lifted something out – a baby – a kid that looked no more than a few months old. She held the child up towards Dillon Teasdale; they spoke together then, blond head almost touching the red-gold one. Then, throwing back her head and laughing, she placed the baby back in the buggy.

What happened next shocked him. Teasdale drew the girl into his arms and started kissing her, and she responded as though it wasn't the first time he'd done that.

Patric felt his stomach turning over. His first thought was for Cass. Did she know something was going on between those two?

He shook his head to try and clear it. She couldn't know, could she? She and Dillon had seemed so close – such good friends. More than friends even – hadn't she allowed the young biker to hug and kiss her that day…?

'Hell!' he muttered as a thought hit him. 'He's two-timing Cass – Cass, of all people. He's making a complete fool of her.'

He couldn't move; couldn't go into the pub now; all

thought of food had deserted him. No! He had to have it out with Teasdale.

'The rat. The two-timing, scheming little rat.'

He set off at a run across the square, determined to give Teasdale either one of two things – a telling off, or else a punch on the jaw.

The girl saw him coming. She pushed Teasdale away from her, swung the baby buggy round and started to race back towards the trees beyond the barriers as if all the hounds of hell were on her heels.

Dillon Teasdale watched her for a moment, then slowly turned round to face Patric as he walked up to him.

'What the hell are you playing at?' Patric demanded, coming to a halt a mere two feet away from him.

'Me?' Teasdale's unshaven stubble and spiked blonde hair made him seem very young to Patric.

'Yes, you! Does Cass know about *her*? The girl who just made a quick getaway?' Patric demanded in a voice like crushed ice.

'Greer? You're talking about Greer Stuart?' Dillon looked bemused.

'Yes. If that's her name. Does Cass know you're playing around with somebody else? Two timing *her*?'

'Look,' Dillon turned belligerent. 'It's no damn business of yours what I do, so just keep out of this, will you, man?'

'You bastard. Cass doesn't deserve to be treated like that.' Patric swung at him.

Dillon lifted a leather-clad arm and deflected the blow. 'Hey – easy now – what the hell are you talking about? What's this got to do with Cass?'

Patric backed off, ashamed of himself, and knowing that he was acting out of character. He couldn't remember the last time he'd resorted to violence of this kind – it must have been in the school playground, he reasoned, when he was ten or eleven years old …

But he couldn't stand by and see Cass get hurt – even though it almost tore his heart out, knowing she was attracted to another man.

It wasn't right. He had to get that through to the young biker. He held up a warning finger. 'Don't play with fire,' he said, his voice aggressive. 'Just don't you hurt that girl.'

Dillon Teasdale looked utterly perplexed. 'I don't hurt women, Mister flippin-Faulkner. I get *my* thrills kicking bikes. And Greer – well, she's just a mate – nothing serious.'

'Just don't …' Patric was breathing hard now. 'Just don't play around with Cass's feelings. I'm telling you – she deserves better than that.'

Dillon looked at him through smoky eyes. 'I thought you were supposed to be the expert on racing bikes around here,' he said. 'Not the damned counsellor for lonely hearts.'

Patric realised he was getting nowhere. He also knew that rattling cages never did any good – it only brought the lion out to see if his dinner was ready.

He backed off, hearing a sound behind him and turned to see Cass hurrying towards them.

'What's wrong?' There was alarm in her face. 'What's going on here?'

Patric wiped the sweat off his upper lip with the back of his hand. How could he tell her? How could he see her expression turn to one of hurt and anguish if he toppled the idol off his column?

Dillon spoke first. 'It's nothing, Cass. Nothing for you to get steamed up about anyway. The guy just saw me with Greer …'

Patric's hackles rose. She had a right to know. 'Tell her the truth,' he blazed. 'Tell her, or I will.'

'Man – you've got the wrong impression altogether.' Dillon looked at Cass and lifted his shoulders in a helpless shrug.

'He was kissing the girl.' Patric rounded on her. 'He's two-timing you, Cass. Hell – it looked to me as if she has a baby too. And I suspect he's the father.'

Cass's voice sounded faint and far away. 'A baby..?' Her eyes held a haunted expression. 'Dillon…' she whispered. 'Dillon, what's been going on here? What have you done?'

Dillon Teasdale's glance ricocheted from one to the other of them as he said, 'Cass – don't get the wrong idea!' and Patric detected a note of warning in the biker's tone.

'The wrong idea!' Patric's laughter was harsh. 'He's got a *child*, Cass – and all the time, he's been making up to you.'

'Me?' Her eyes widened; she seemed to have lost the power to say anything more.

Dillon broke in. 'Mister Faulkner was in the pub and came racing over – scaring Greer half to death. So much so, that she shot off before I could introduce either her *or* the baby to him.'

'Not before I *saw* that baby.' Patric's voice was grim. 'That's why I came rushing over here. Cass has a right to know that you've fathered a child, Teasdale. And by that 'Greer' woman …'

'OK!' Dillon held up a hand. 'OK – I confess.' He looked wildly at Cass. 'Greer had the baby with her, Cass. *My* baby … you understand?'

Patric's hand shot out and hauled Dillon round to face him.

'You rat!' he snarled. 'You're nothing but a bastard – playing up to Cass while you've got that girl in the family way. You should be ashamed of yourself!'

'Aw, man. It's not the end of the world,' Dillon groaned. 'It happens. And do you have to be so bloody old-fashioned? "*In the family way*"…? I ask you! Nobody calls it that nowadays. One-parent families aren't anything to write home about. It happens all the time.'

'Leave him alone,' Cass said weakly, shooting a strange glance at Patric that made him let go of Dillon.

'Cass, he's making a laughing stock of you.' Patric was still fuming inwardly. He couldn't understand why she was taking this all so calmly. 'If he's got a child, he should be marrying the girl – not playing around with you as well.'

'Dillon and Greer are both good friends of mine,' she said. 'I *do* know about the baby, Patric.'

He stood still and stared at her. 'You do?'

She nodded and glared at Dillon.

It seemed to Patric as if the atmosphere was so thick, it could be cut through with a knife. He waited for Cass to say something, but she didn't, and she was now carefully not looking at Dillon Teasdale.

Dillon seemed a hundred per cent composed, however, and said in a matter of fact voice, 'Of course she knows about the baby. She plays 'auntie' to little Tiff, don't you, Cass? Baby-sits for us sometimes when Greer and I go out at nights on a date.'

Cass, Patric saw, was breathing shallowly; she said in a weak voice, 'I – I have Tiffany at nights – she stays with me.'

Patric still wasn't convinced. There was something wrong. Some undercurrent that he couldn't quite put his finger on. One of them was lying, he was sure of that. But who? And why?

'Leave it, will you?' Cass said, 'Just leave it, Patric.

You're making something out of nothing.'

Dillon winked at her, and said, 'That's right, love. You tell him. Put him in his place, eh?'

Patric felt like flooring him. 'No!' He held up a warning finger in front of Dillon's nose. 'You listen to me. You do the right thing by that girl, my lad, or else I'll …'

'You'll what, mate?' Dillon seemed amused.

'I'll take that smirk off your face for one thing. It's not clever to get a girl pregnant …'

Dillon shoved both hands into his leather bike jacket and said, 'Hit me then. I dare you.'

Cass stepped between them. 'No violence,' she said quietly. 'Please – let's all drop this, shall we? Let's behave like civilised adults.'

'Come with me, Cass.' Patric was more controlled now. 'Come on – let me take you for a drink before filming starts again. I expect you could do with one – and a bite to eat.'

She shook her head. 'No thanks. I've arranged to meet someone for lunch.'

Patric stared at her. Dillon gave a smothered cough, then said, 'Want a lift, love? I could take you on the bike?'

Patric's hands clenched into fists at his side.

Cass said quickly, 'No, thanks. I've got my car back. I took it down to the garage in the village this morning to have a couple of new tyres fitted.'

Dillon grinned. 'Maybe I'll join you. You and your date.'

'Please yourself.' To Patric's ears she sounded weary.

He lunged forward, 'Cass – please wait …'

'No,' she said. 'I can't. Trent wants me back here for two o'clock and already I'm late.'

'For your date?' he grated, while Dillon tried unsuccess-fully to smother a laugh.

She looked at him squarely. 'Yes,' she said. 'And I think

you'd better get off for some lunch, Patric. Trent wants us to start at two o'clock sharp, this afternoon, and you know what a stickler he is.'

Dillon swung round. 'Well,' he said, 'I'm off to join the lads.' He winked again at Cass, making Patric's blood boil at his nonchalant attitude. 'See you around, mate.'

The wink this time was directed at Patric, and then Dillon started back across the square, shoulders set and arms swinging in a jaunty fashion; back to where his beloved Harley was parked with the rest of the bikes.

Patric waited till he was out of ear-shot, then he shook his head at Cass and said coldly, 'You don't care, do you? You just don't care that he got that girl into trouble and left her with a baby to bring up on her own?'

'It's not my problem.' She stared hard at him. 'And it's not yours either, Patric.'

'I don't understand you,' he said. 'You never used to be like this, Cass.'

'No?' Her head jerked up. She met his eyes without flinching.

'No,' he said. 'You were once such a caring girl.'

She gave him a quick smile, then looked at her watch. 'I really do have to be going,' she said. 'I told you – I'm late already.'

He watched her walk away towards where her car was parked, and still he couldn't understand how she could have changed so much. She just didn't seem to care that Dillon Teasdale could behave so heartlessly towards that girl with the baby.

She got in the car and started up the engine, and never even looked at him. And he had to watch helplessly as she drove away, out of the village, down the road between the high rocks and the trees, and out of his sight.

chapter thirteen

As Trent and Patric left the 'Lead Miner' pub some time later, Trent said, 'Will ya take a look at that Harley, Patric? That kid – Teasdale – he's not happy about the compression stroke or the damned timing. He says the wheel alignment's all wrong too. In fact, according to our friend Teasdale, just about *everything* is wrong with the machine, so I'd like you to take a look. Pronto! OK?'

'I need to have a word with Cass first.'

'No can do, buddy. Sandie's gone. Called me on her mobile a while back – just before you came into the pub. A headache, she said. Y'know though, I've never known Sandie have a headache before. And, while we're on the subject, will you *please* call her Sandie and not Cass. It gets confusing.'

'Gone where? What do you mean, she's gone? I was talking to her just before lunch. She was OK then.'

Trent lifted his shoulders again. 'Well, she's gone back home, I expect. Heck, man,' he added, 'I don't know. She seemed in a hurry to get off the phone, that's all I do know. Women are like that though, aren't they. Headaches seem to come on for no particular reason. Right?'

'But I have to see her!'

'You have that Harley to see to first.'

'There's nothing wrong with it. Teasdale is just being a bore. He and I don't hit it off. I tell you, Trent, he's just being awkward and making trouble for trouble's sake.'

'On your head be it then if anything *does* go wrong. I

don't want no hold-ups with rehearsals this afternoon. I want to get on with the damn film. Delays mean dollars. Know what I mean?'

'The Harley's OK,' Patric insisted. 'I inspected it this morning. Dillon Teasdale is being precocious. Anyone would think that he was the star of this show, instead of just being an extra who never even gets his face on screen.'

'OK, OK.' Trent held up a hand placatingly.

'So, tell me where Cass is right now, huh.'

'Where she lives, man? Rydale Tor. The little place with the big rocks, a few miles south of here. OK? That's where I assumed she was going, anyhow. I don't know that she has a home anywhere else, man.'

'Rydale Tor.' Patric's face was grim. 'So she *does* live there.'

'I thought you knew. I could have told you any time. She has this little place with a sales shop underneath the flat. It's on the main street. She's intent on setting herself up there – as a photographer when she's through with the lot of *us*. I told her – get writing more screenplays, girl. That's where the money is. But no. She's digging her heels in. She doesn't want to be different. She wants to take pictures for a living.' Trent shook his head. 'She's crazy, man. I told her so.'

Patric was in a hurry to be gone. 'Look – you don't need me. I'll be back tomorrow.'

'Aw, don't be like that. Just take a peek at that Harley.'

'Dillon Teasdale knows as much as I do about bikes. Get him to take a look himself. I'm not on your payroll, Trent, so I don't think I have to ask permission for a few hours off, do you?'

Patric didn't wait for an answer as he quickly sprinted across the square to where his car was parked. The only thought filling his mind was Cass. And he knew he had to see her; he had to talk to her and get this Teasdale problem sorted out – once and for all.

Was it really a headache, he wondered? Or was that just an excuse she'd used to get away because of what he'd told her about Dillon and that girl with the baby?

One thing was certain. He was going to find out – especially now he knew for certain where it was she lived.

The phone was ringing upstairs as Cass let herself in by the front door. She ran up to answer it and it was Trent.

'Sandie-baby. Is everything OK?'

Out of breath from hurrying, she answered, 'Yes. I'm sorry I had to dash off like that.'

'Don't bother coming back today.'

She glanced at the clock on her kitchen wall and gave a little laugh. It was well past two o'clock. 'I wasn't going to.'

'That's good. Sandie – I had to ring you. You're going to get a visitor, and I thought it best to warn you. I didn't know if he'd be welcome or not?'

She drew in her breath. 'What are you talking about, Trent?'

'Patric. He was quite put out. Said he wanted to talk to you. Wanted to know where you lived and I just blurted it out. Hope I haven't gone and landed you in the fu… well you know what, Sandie – me and my big mouth. Guess I should have been more careful, but…'

'Hell!'

'From the sound of that four-letter word, I guess I *have* landed you in it.' For once, Trent sounded subdued. 'Gee, Sandie – I'm real sorry. I just never thought – and the guy was so insistent.'

Cass's temper flared. 'Look – I don't need this. My personal details are my affair. You had absolutely no right to tell *anybody* where I live – especially Patric Faulkner. I just don't want to see him right now.'

'Sandie-baby…'

'Oh – oh – Trent,' she stormed, '*Why* did you have to tell *him*?'

'Because he asked, sweetheart. And how was I to know…'

'To know what?' Suddenly she was wary. Just what had Patric been saying about her, she wondered?

'Look – I put two-and-two together. OK? Patric didn't say anything. Seems like I've caught on to something about you two though, huh? There always seems a sort of atmosphere when the pair of you get together.'

'Trent – I could kill you!' she seethed.

'That's right, baby. You just do that.' She heard him laugh. 'If it makes you feel better, you go right ahead and pull the damn trigger. I guess I deserve it.'

'Damn! Hell! Fuzz and furoré!' Cass swore as she put down the phone, before flying around the flat, picking up bits of baby-rusk, cuddly toys, talcum-powder and a pack of disposable nappies.. She hoovered, dusted, wiped down Tiff's high chair then bundled it into the baby's bedroom and closed the door on it.

At last, she looked round the spotlessly clean living-room, making sure it was now a baby-free zone. She let out a long breath, picked up her hands-free phone and dialled the number of the mobile she'd bought for Greer to carry around with her. As she waited for Greer to answer, she watched the road through the window. There was no sign yet of a big blue car.

She flopped down on the window seat, leaning her arm

across the back of it where she could still watch the road as Greer answered the insistent bleeping.

'Hi, Cass.'

Cass explained what was happening. 'Look, love, I know I said I'd have a cup of tea waiting for you when you'd done your bit of shopping, but something's happened. Aaron Trent, the idiot, has given Patric my address, and Patric's hot-footing it over here right now. You're not anywhere near the flat at the moment, are you?'

'I'm still in the High Street, Cass – but right at the other end of Rydale Tor. Tiff's awake. I was going to take her for a good long walk, but then I thought I'd better bring her back as it's nearly her tea-time.'

'Don't bring her back.' Panic made her voice rise. 'Look – Patric will be here at any minute. For heaven's sake, keep Tiff out of the way – just for a couple of hours. He mustn't see her. He mustn't even suspect that I've got a baby.'

'Is it OK if I take her and show her off to my Mum? You know where I live – quite a walk from the centre of Rydale Tor – but…'

Cass's mind was working overtime. 'Yes, love. Anything. I'm in a panic here. I can't risk Patric finding out about Tiff. But about her tea… Well, she really will need something to eat in the next half hour or so.'

'Don't worry, Cass. I'll pop in the chemist's shop and get her something in a packet or a pot. She likes those apricot and rice things. I'll make myself scarce then. Mum will be over the moon having a baby to look after for a couple of hours.'

'After this morning's little fracas between Dillon and Patric, I'll have to be on my guard,' Cass said.

Greer chuckled. 'You really are in a panic, aren't you? But don't worry. I can assure you that Patric didn't get even a glimpse of Tiff close-up this morning. I was out of there like a bat out of hell when I saw him coming towards us – leaving poor old Dillon to face the music.'

Cass heard a car pulling up on the road outside, looked down through the window and saw it was a familiar dark blue one. The panic started all over again. 'Hell! He's here. I've got to go. Two hours – Greer. Just give me two hours or so – till around five o'clock, let's say. I'll make sure he's gone by then, OK?'

'OK, Cass. Best of luck.'

She put the phone down to a thunderous hammering on the door downstairs. Knowing immediately who it must be, Cass took several deep breaths before going down to let Patric in.

'So – this is where you live. Not Manchester.'

'I never said I lived in Manchester.' She stood stony-faced, holding on to the door, and glared at him.

'I don't know why you thought you had to lie to me.'

She said nothing.

'Can I come in?'

She pulled the door open a little. 'I suppose so – if you must.'

'Upstairs?' he enquired in his politest voice, glancing obliquely at the large empty space that was to be her studio through the open door that led off from the little hallway at the bottom of the stairs. 'I take it that's where you intend making your living after the filming's finished.'

'Trent's been talking out of turn, I take it! And not for the first time.' She nodded and closed the door to the outside.

He waited for her to lead the way. She took him into the sitting room when they reached her living quarters.

'Nice,' he said. 'Cosy. A lot like the house you shared

with your mother in Suffolk.'

Cass remained standing, her hands on her hips and said, 'What do you want?'

'Tea would be nice.'

He was maddeningly cool, while inside *she* was burning and bubbling. It was on the tip of her tongue to tell him to make the tea himself, and then she remembered, Tiff's feeding bottle sterilising unit was on one of the worktops in the kitchen. 'Sit down,' she said. 'I'll put the kettle on to boil.'

'Want me to help?'

She spun round. 'No. Sit down.'

'Cass…' He was still standing. He held out a hand to her but she ignored it and turned away.

She went through to the kitchen and started to make the tea. How different to the cosy, old-fashioned kitchen of the Victorian farmhouse where she and Patric had once lived and been so wonderfully happy together. So many times she'd dreamed of being back there, with the man she'd loved so much, sitting at the large scrubbed pine table and warming her toes in front of the comforting red Aga cooker…

'Cass…?'

Patric's voice suddenly broke into her reverie, jerking her roughly back to the harsh present. Swiftly, she whirled round to face him as he walked towards her.

'Damn! I told you to wait for me in the other room. I *told* you to sit down.' She was flustered. 'I haven't cleaned properly in here today…' her mind was whirling around and around. She had to find an excuse – any excuse at all, to get him out of there so he wouldn't see the steriliser.

He'd seen it. He walked over to it and gazed down at it. 'I didn't really believe the bit about you baby-sitting for

Teasdale and his girlfriend. But, I now see that I was wrong.'

Weakly, she said, 'You should trust people a bit more, Patric. Dillon isn't an out and out liar, yet you dislike him for some reason.'

'I thought he was lying – until I saw this.' He pointed at the sterilising unit, and smiled across the kitchen at her. 'I suppose you keep a couple of feeding bottles in – just in case they dump the kid on you?'

She nodded, unable to speak because she was afraid her voice would sound squeaky and unreal. Her throat was dry, her legs were shaking. She hated lies and deceit of any kind, but now she knew just how easy it was to start lying.

'You shouldn't let them put on you, Cass. You're young. You don't want tying down with somebody else's baby.'

'They don't *put on me*.' Just say as little as possible, she told herself, and tried to convince herself that it wasn't *really* a lie if she did that. It didn't work. She still felt guilty. In the past, she'd never had secrets from him. She'd never told even a little white lie either. It left a nasty taste in her mouth doing it now.

'Have you got a sore throat or something?'

Quickly she shook her head. 'Just been talking a lot today, I guess.'

The kettle began to boil and she waited till it clicked off then poured water into the teapot.

He came up close to her. 'Here, let me help – where do you keep your cups?'

'It's OK. Really.' Panic again! In the cupboard where she kept the crockery were little plastic feeding cups, a Pooh-bear plate and dish. A bowl that had '*Tiffany*' printed round the edge of it, which Greer had bought from a local pottery. There were spare feeding bottles, a bottle brush. And if he happened to open the wrong cupboard door, one of the lower ones, he'd see packets of disposable nappies, and cans and packets of baby food. He'd be suspicious then, at so much evidence of a baby living there. 'Please Patric,' she said weakly, 'just go and sit down. I can manage.'

'I want to be near you.'

She turned to face him. The old magic was working again. His nearness was closing in on her, she could feel the pull of him, hear the quiet magnetism in his voice, see his smile, as he drew her into his arms.

'No…' she whispered. 'No… this isn't right.'

His mouth clamped down on her lips, silencing her, and she knew she was lost and helpless to fight against him. She didn't want to fight him though; she wanted to hold him and love him and never let him go again.

His hands were in her hair, holding her face immobile. She could feel his fingers digging into her scalp – almost as if he would hold her there by force – as if he thought she might try to fly away from him.

She closed her eyes, gave herself up to the glorious sensation of having him touch her, and run those hard fingers through her long silky hair while his lips were doing all manner of strange things to that rigid resolve she'd built up inside her over the past months – the resolve to forget him, to have nothing more to do with him. That tight, wound-up spring that had been inside her ever since he'd come to Derbyshire too, was slowly relaxing now. It was melting away as if it had never existed as she pressed herself close up against his body and tried to become a part of him.

She reached up and clasped her hands round the back of his neck and then shuddered in silent wicked torment as he started a slow exploration of her body with *his* hands. She'd forgotten what it could be like – loving a man like this. She'd become a mother and had pushed all thoughts of being a *woman* right out of her mind.

He buried his face in the sweetness of her hair. She heard him draw in his breath and murmur. 'The same perfume. The same body scent. Cass – I've missed you so much.'

Michelle, she thought weepily, Michelle had been on the receiving end of all this.

His hand came up to her throat, stroking her and holding her face so he could look into her eyes. She averted her gaze. 'What was that for?' he asked gently.

'What?' She tried not to look at him, but he forced her head round so she had to.

'I suddenly felt you going away from me,' he said. 'You forget, Cass – I know you so well. I know every little move you make, I know what kind of thoughts are going through your head. Everything was all right until just now… a second ago.'

'Michelle,' she whispered in a husky voice. 'I was thinking about Michelle.'

'Thinking *what* about Michelle?'

'That she's had you while I…'

Both hands were holding her face now, close to his own. His eyes were staring down into her eyes. She could feel his breath fanning her cheek as he said, 'Michelle hasn't had me. I swear it, Cass. I haven't touched her in years.'

Her eyes were wide and pleading. 'You wouldn't lie to me about something so important, would you…?'

'I'm not lying. I've never lied to you.'

His hands slid down to rest on her arms. He shook her gently. 'She isn't my wife any longer,' he said. 'Michelle and I have no future together. I haven't lived with her in ages, Cass. I would *never* lie to you about that.'

She swallowed painfully, trying to keep the tears at bay, but they overflowed and trickled down her cheeks. He leaned forward and kissed them, then flicked his tongue out and licked them away. He kissed her eyes then, and tangled his hands in her hair and she hung onto him, and gave herself up to his kisses and his murmurings and the thousand and one little things that she loved about him – the fine, prickly stubble that could hardly be seen – just felt, the dark shadow just beginning to show along his top lip, the firmness of his hands, the long, lean line of his body. And the part of him that told her of his need, the hard-swelling thrust against her lower body that was reminding her all too forcibly of all those other bitter-sweet times they'd made love.

She wanted him so much. It had been such a long time since this special need had erupted inside her. She was burning up for him, and all her agonising was over. He was here and she was here, and there was nothing to stop them...

The journey from kitchen to bedroom seemed like one small step – one tiny movement that in the blink of an eye had them standing beside Cass's huge old-fashioned double bed that had been transported up from Suffolk when she'd moved to Derbyshire.

She was naked; Patric was naked. Their clothes lay bunched together in an untidy heap on the floor. She didn't care. She luxuriated in the silk of his skin, the sheen of his flesh. He tumbled her onto the bed and her laughter was that of the old days when they'd first learned to love the touch of each other. She lay back on the thick duvet, sinking into its softness, and he leaned on his elbow and gazed down into her eyes, his own dark and mysterious, a little smile playing around his lips.

'Now I have you back – the real Cass. Naked and unashamed.' He bent and kissed the tip of her nose.

'Am I only real when I'm naked?' Her eyes were alight with love of him.

'You'd changed when I found you again.' He lifted a strand of her hair and let it drizzle through his fingers. 'You've grown your hair. You wear bright colours.'

'You don't like the change?'

Kissing her again, he said, 'I absolutely love the change. You look gorgeous in that rainbow coloured shirt.'

'So why did you take it off?' she teased.

'So it wouldn't crease,' he said in a serious voice. 'And also so that I wouldn't tear the buttons off in a mad frenzy, when I made love to you.'

'Mad frenzy, huh?' Her hands were linked at the back of his neck. She loosed them now and trailed her fingers down over his shoulders, then smoothed her hands across his chest, circling the dark hairs that grew short and thick on his body, she whispered, 'Show me the mad frenzy,' and she raised the top half of her body so she could press her lips to his throat, and then work her way up to his chin, and then his lips…

'Cass – I want to marry you,' he said, his mouth on hers.

Happiness soared inside her. She wanted to tell him then and there about Tiffany – but it could wait, she decided, it could wait for half an hour or so…

The world receded; what did they need with the world anyway? All that mattered was what lay contained in that little square island of bed. Her breasts peaked at his touch, she fell back into cloudy softness and knew again the searing, breathtaking ecstasy that she'd once taken so much for granted as he found that secret part of her he knew so well, and that only he could touch and bring to life. He brought her to heart-stopping heights of passion which were mingled with love and longing and aching for him. And when she reached a point in her universe where everything was about to explode, he entered her body and made her cry out with the first, thrusting release of everything she had ever dreamed about, lived for, and hoped would happen again.

The return to earth, to the world, was as gentle as thistledown floating down on stillest air. She drifted into sleep, thinking she must tell him about Tiffany; holding tightly to his hand and allowing herself the luxury of just lying there for a few moments, before slipping into a drowsy state; unaware of the shadows lengthening outside.

More than a couple of hours must have passed, when Patric woke and heard a sound in the next room. Stirring, he sat up in the bed, frowning. Somebody was singing softly although Cass was still sleeping soundly beside him. He eased off the bed carefully, dragged on his jeans and shirt, ran his fingers through his hair and went over to the door, and listened.

Somebody was moving around in another part of the flat. He could hear them in the kitchen now, running water.

He looked at his watch. Six thirty! Six thirty in the evening. What the hell was going on?

He turned to look at Cass, curled up on the bed. Ought he to wake her?

He decided against it. Quietly he opened the door, went through it, and then closed it almost silently behind him. The living-room door was just down the passage – next door to Cass's bedroom and another room at the back of the house. There were two other doors on the opposite side of the passage. He pushed one open. A bathroom. He crept to the next one, pushed that one too.

His breath came in a sharp gasp. It was a nursery, a small room with pink paper on the walls and white cupboards and drawers. There was a cot, a mobile of dogs and cats hanging from the ceiling. A lamp shaped like a flying saucer with coloured figures inside it. He twisted the top slightly; it played a gentle lullaby.

He backed out of the room, closed the door again, then went across the passage to the living-room, mystified as to why Cass should have gone to such trouble to provide a nursery, merely for a friend's baby.

There was a girl there. She was standing by the window with a baby in her arms. He recognised her as the girl that Dillon Teasdale had been mauling on the film set that day.

She was standing in profile and hadn't heard him. For a second, he was angry with her for intruding. Why should Cass have to befriend her to this extent? Why had she turned over one of her rooms to the child? Just what was Dillon Teasdale to her that she could open up her home to his girlfriend and his brat of a child?

He made a deliberate sound, a small cough at the back of his throat.

Greer Stuart whirled round to face him. The baby was cradled in one arm. Her free hand flew to her mouth. 'Heck! You scared me. I thought Cass had gone out – the place was so quiet.'

'You have a key?'

She nodded, but seemed disinclined to say anything more.

He walked across to her; she pushed the child up against her shoulder so that only its back view was visible to him. Gently, he said, 'Let me see the baby.'

Her eyes were wide and terrified. 'No! No!'

He held out a hand. 'Don't be scared. I saw you earlier today with that lad who has the motorbike. Let me see the baby. Is it a girl? I saw the nursery.' He gave a twisted smile. 'Pink's usually for a girl, isn't it?'

She was looking beyond him now, over his shoulder. He half-turned and saw Cass coming across the living-room carpet. Her feet were bare but she was wearing a short, pale-pink towelling bathrobe.

She stopped when she saw the girl with the baby, ran her fingers through her tousled hair and said, 'Heck! I didn't realise the time…'

'You said two hours, Cass.' The girl glanced at him, then back at Cass. 'And it's more than three, I thought…' her voice tailed away.

Patric was somewhere between the two of them. He didn't know who to look at and who to ignore. He looked at Cass's face. It almost mirrored the girls – eyes wide, but not scared as Greer's were. No! What he saw in Cass's eyes as she looked at the baby was a very different expression altogether.

'It doesn't matter, Greer,' she said gently.

'Somebody tell me…' he said. 'Somebody explain.'

Cass spoke first. Her words were aimed at the girl. 'It's all right, Greer. Let Patric see her.'

And carefully, Greer turned Tiffany around to face the tall, dark-haired man who was her father.

chapter fourteen

Patric looked at the baby's face and it seemed to him as if he were gazing into a mirror and seeing his own eyes and his own wayward dark hair. Pouting, unsmiling lips warned him that Tiffany was wary of him however.

There was no question about it. The baby was his own flesh and blood, and he felt as if he'd been dealt a physical blow from which he'd never recover. This was his child – his baby. It was something so perfect that he felt humbled and yet, at the same time, delighted. Nothing in his life before had made him feel so proud, so joyous that he wanted to yell it out to all the world that this perfect piece of mankind was his, and the jigsaw of his life was falling into place.

He held out his arms towards Greer and the baby, and saw the girl glancing at Cass before handing Tiffany over to him. Greer had disappeared when he next looked up, and from somewhere far off, he heard the sound of the down-stairs door being closed.

He turned round to Cass then, with Tiffany held carefully on one arm, while with the other he supported her back. It was a strange feeling to him, holding this little mite; he couldn't ever remember holding a baby in his life before, yet suddenly it felt so natural. He had never felt so protec-tive of any human being before. She was soft and smelled like a baby. She was a part of him and a part of Cass and love welled up in him, love and a desire to protect her and wake up every morning knowing she was there, and go to bed at night knowing she was safe. She was his baby and he felt a huge grin plastering itself all over his face as again he drank in her perfection and her prettiness.

Cass was still standing where she'd been when Greer had been with them. She hadn't moved a step further towards him, and now he saw there was a deep well of anxiety in her eyes, a taut expression on her face, and it hurt him to think she could actually be afraid of him – or, rather, afraid of what he might be feeling and thinking after the shock he'd just had.

'You should have told me,' he said. 'Cass – I should have been there for you. You shouldn't have had to go through this on your own. Why the hell didn't you tell me you were pregnant?' And the joy inside him reverberated through his words. He felt that he'd never stop smiling, he felt as if he'd just been handed the greatest gift on earth.

She made a useless kind of movement with her hands. 'How could I tell you? Just at that time you had other things on your mind.'

'Michelle,' he said, with a note of disgust in his voice. 'Do you think Michelle would have taken priority over *this*?' He glanced down at the baby and touched his lips to her downy soft hair. Tiffany reached out two tiny hands and grasped at his chin, chuckling as his hours-old stubble prickled her fingers. 'Cass…' he looked up at her again, 'Cass…' his gaze returned again to the baby. He was entranced by her. 'Cass – she is so marvellous. How on earth did we manage to produce something as perfect as this?'

He walked over to her and stood very close. He was absorbed with the baby and laughed into Tiffany's face as she jigged up and down on his arm. 'Look at those lashes – they're just like yours, except darker, and the way she turns her head, her chin tilting up – just like you, my darling – feisty, an independent little cuss, even at this early age.'

Cass gave a soft little laugh. 'I take it you approve of her then.'

'Approve? Cass – I'm so proud of her. It's a shock – but the best kind of shock I've ever had. But I feel bad about you having to face it all on your own – the pregnancy, the birth…' he felt dazed. 'Heck – the things I've missed out on…'

She rested a hand on his arm. 'But not anymore. She's your daughter, Patric – and she's getting to the age where she needs to know she has a daddy.'

He looked dazed again. 'I don't even know how old she *is*?' he said. He glanced up at her again, realising he was paying far too much attention to the baby and not enough to *her*.

'She'll soon be seven-months-old. She was born on the twenty-ninth of November – on one of the coldest days ever, when Rydale Tor was cut off from the outside world by snowdrifts.'

At once he was concerned. 'What happened?'

'I only managed to get as far as the local cottage hospital.' She grinned. 'It was lovely and homely – I wasn't the first – and I don't suppose I'll be the last to give birth there, but it just felt right. D'you know what I mean? No high-tech equipment, no high-rise delivery suites, just a bed in a little side room on the ground floor where nurses and patients kept popping in and chatting to me. There were no complications so I was up and about in no time at all.'

He reached up with the hand that had supported Tiff's back – but which he now realised wasn't needed – and stroked Cass's hair back from her face. 'Did you think of me?'

'Constantly!' She grimaced. 'Once it was all over though I forgave you and wondered if you'd like her name – I wondered too if you'd have preferred a boy to a girl…'

'They say little girls cling to their fathers more than boys, don't they?' He wanted her affirmation on this. Already in the space of a few short minutes, some instinct inside him wanted to protect baby Tiffany, and as she dozed in his arms and nuzzled up to him, her head drooping against his shoulder, he knew that this was a precious moment in time that he would never forget.

She nodded. 'I don't remember much about my own father; he died when I was young, but I do remember feeling lost and left out when the other girls at school talked about their daddies and I didn't have one.'

'What do I do with her when she's asleep like this.' He kept his voice to a low whisper. 'Will she wake if I move?'

Cass laughed softly. 'I wouldn't think so. You can go and sit down on the couch with her – or you can lie her on the cushions there and just keep watch over her if you'd rather.'

'I want to keep watch over her for the rest of my life.' He gave her a direct look of understanding before turning away and taking Tiffany to the couch and lying her down where she could stretch out her little legs and arms, and yawn widely before settling in sleep again.

He stood looking down at the baby then, and Cass came up and linked her arm through his. He bent his head and kissed her hair.

She tilted her face up to his. 'Keep an eye on her while I have a shower, huh?'

His smile reached his eyes. 'Of course.'

He watched as she padded back across the room and went towards the bathroom. She understood that he needed time alone with Tiffany, he realised. He carried a dining chair over to where the baby lay and sat on it where he could watch her, not daring to perch even on the edge of the couch lest he should wake her.

It was after midnight when Patric got back to the bungalow on the moors the other side of Buxton, and he let himself in quietly and switched on the hall light. He still felt as if he had a huge grin on his face, and thoughts of Cass and the baby still filled his mind to the exclusion of all else.

'What time do you call this?' Silently, Michelle had emerged from the shadows of the hall to confront him and he felt irritated by her presence. He wanted to be alone, to think about Cass and the baby; Michelle was an obstacle he could well do without. She treated him all the time now as if they were still married and it was time, he decided, to put a stop to it. Pity was all very well in its place, but Michelle had got things all out of proportion, and he, he realised, had done little to stop her.

He glanced at his watch. 'It's twelve twenty. Is that a problem?'

'Don't try to be clever with me. You've been with *her*, haven't you?'

'Have I?' he asked mildly, then knowing he'd get no peace until she'd interrogated him completely, he went on, 'Yes, I've been with Cass. I presume you're referring to Cass when you speak of '*her*' in such a derogatory manner?'

She almost flinched away from him as he passed her in the corridor and headed for his own bedroom. She yelled after him, 'You have no right…'

'To stay out after my normal bed-time?' He spared her a glance as he reached his door, raising his brows to enquire, 'I didn't realise a curfew had been imposed. Didn't realise also that you had the right to impose restrictions on my time.'

He saw her swallow and, for a moment, he felt sorry for her. She wasn't lost for words for long however. 'Don't talk to me like that. I was only concerned for you,' she snapped, 'I thought you might have been involved in an accident or something. You aren't usually this late.'

His hand fell from the door latch. He faced her fully. 'And if there had been an accident? What then?'

'I – I *am* your wife. I do worry…'

'You are *not* my wife, Michelle. When are you going to accept that our marriage is over? We've been divorced now for more than five years.'

'You're still here with me though.' There was an arrogant tilt to her head, the ghost of a triumphant smile on her lips. She moved awkwardly on her crutches, towards him, and came up close. 'You'd never leave me, Patric. We had so much going for us at one time. And it could be like that again…'

He gave a short laugh. 'No way.' He wondered whether to tell her about Tiffany, then thought better of it. If she knew he had a daughter, she'd move heaven and earth to keep him and Cass apart. He knew her well. She could be a vindictive bitch. His eyes narrowed slightly as she spoke again.

'I never wanted our marriage to end, Patric.…' She made a movement with her hands. 'I never really wanted a divorce – it wasn't the answer to our problems.'

His temper, already frayed by her presence, finally snapped. 'Hell and damnation, what do you think you'll achieve by all this maudlin clinging to the past?'

She didn't seem like her usual self. She sounded somehow frightened when she replied, 'Haven't you ever wanted to turn back the clock – haven't you ever wondered…' her voice tailed off.

'Wondered what?' He was impatient and his tone told her so. He stared at her with hostility in his eyes.

'If we should try again with our marriage – have another shot at it?'

He was weary and couldn't face more arguments, recriminations, and 'what-ifs'! He sighed. 'Oh, no. I've had enough, Michelle. There's nothing left between us now. You know damn well there isn't. You can't resurrect something that's dead.'

'But if I had a baby…' she began.

'Oh, no.' His laughter was harsh. 'There's no question of me ever sharing a bed with you again, Michelle.'

'But it's not too late.' She stood barring the way to his room, leaning heavily on her crutches, staring straight at him, 'Lots of women have babies at my age…'

'Michelle – for me it *is* too late. I don't want to sound cruel, but I've got to be honest and realistic about this. I don't love you any more. And if you'd tell the truth yourself, you'd realise that you don't love me either.'

'We were good together once.'

'A long time ago.' He hesitated for only a moment. 'I meant what I said, I don't love you, Michelle.'

She reeled back from him. 'You did once. You could again. I could change, Patric. I'd do anything…'

'You can't change things,' he said. 'You might pretend that you'd changed yourself, but in reality nothing would be changed, would it? You left me a long time ago, Michelle. You gave yourself to a man nearly ten years younger than yourself. You made an absolute fool of me, and you also made a farce of our marriage.

'Moreover,' he added grimly, 'You *know* that you didn't

love *me*. So, just what could I give you?'

She glanced down at the floor. She was wearing her long, white bathrobe. 'I made a mistake,' she muttered. 'The biggest mistake of my life in thinking I wanted Craig Andrews more than I wanted you.'

He took a step towards her, took hold of her shoulders and shook her. 'Stop play-acting,' he said, making her look directly into his eyes. 'You'd have done anything for Craig Andrews. You were utterly besotted with him. You couldn't have cared less about me. Even when you weren't with Craig, you were lost to me.'

'How do you know that?' Her eyes were tortured.

'I knew,' he said. 'It's just something I *knew*, Michelle. I'm not a fool – and after being married to you for all those years, I know something else too. I know that I can never love you again. I know that I can *never* feel the same way I did about you in the beginning. You killed all that.'

'When I killed Craig Andrews?' She looked up at him. 'Is that what you're saying?'

He shook his head. 'Long before Craig died. It was finished for us, Michelle. Way back.'

'You won't even try for a reconciliation then?'

He let his hands fall away from her and stepped away from her. 'No.'

'Don't you find me even the least bit attractive any more?' Her eyes were pleading with him; the words came straight from her heart.

He hated to hurt her more than she'd already been hurt, but her unhappiness was of her own making and nothing could be gained by leading her on. 'I couldn't even start to make love to you,' he said. 'I just don't feel that way about you any more.'

Her face twisted. 'You sure do know how to hurt me...'

Her voice caught on a sob.

He leaned against the door frame. 'What good does it do to lie?'

'Let me come in and talk to you,' she pleaded. 'Let me come in to your bedroom – I won't make any trouble. I just need to talk.'

'No,' he said, inwardly guessing at her intentions. Once inside his bedroom, it would be hell's own job getting rid of her. He knew now that it had been the biggest mistake ever, feeling sorry for her, giving in to her tears and tantrums these past months. For her sake as well as his own, he should have turned his back on her, left her to make a new life for herself. It hadn't been enough for her though – him finding a housekeeper and a nurse – it had been him she wanted on a string. All along she had known how to manipulate him with her show of helplessness. Now, though, he saw her for what she was – a strong-minded woman who would go all out for what she could get.

She was staring hard at him now, and suddenly he knew. He *knew* with absolute certainty that somehow she'd found out about Tiffany.

But how? And when? And *why* hadn't she said something – taunted him with the knowledge? He felt a cold kind of fear creeping into him and was afraid – for Cass and for the baby. Michelle had killed once and had managed to get away with it, because there had been an element of doubt about whether it was an accident or not. But both he and Michelle knew that it had been no accident.

Dare she attempt something like that again? His hands clenched at his sides. If anyone harmed that baby, or Cass…

He forced down the feelings of fear and uncertainty that were festering inside him. If once she knew she'd rattled him, he'd be done for. She'd hold all the aces.

And she was a dangerous woman.

'I think it's time you went home to Suffolk,' he said. 'I never should have brought you here.'

She was suddenly quiet and her face took on a closed and cold look. 'I've lost you then.'

'We lost each other, Michelle. A long time ago.'

'I've got something to tell you then. If you won't make love to me.'

'To tell me?'

She'd clamped her lips shut.

'So go on,' he said. 'Tell me.'

'I've missed a period.' She couldn't meet his gaze.

He drew in a sharp breath, unable to reply to her. He hadn't expected this, even knowing about her and Trent. He'd have put money on it that Trent, at least, would have taken precautions. The man wasn't a fool…

'Look at me,' he said quietly. 'Look at me and tell me straight, Michelle.'

'I did a pregnancy test. I know it's early days, but…' she shrugged.

'It was… positive?' he asked.

She nodded, then lifted her head and looked straight at him. 'We could pretend to the world that the baby was yours,' she said. 'We could start again, Patric – a new life…'

'With me admitting another man's child was my own?' He was incredulous that she should think it would be so easy or acceptable to him.

'It was just a thought.' She looked away again. 'We'd be a proper family, you see, and as a family, it would be a brand new start for us.'

'Do I need to ask who the father is? Has there been more than one man in your life recently?'

'I'm not a slut,' she responded swiftly.

'Aren't you?' His tone was mild.

Again her head jerked up and her eyes were blazing now. 'No more of a slut than Cass Fairburn was when she was expecting your brat, I suppose.'

'So you know about that? You know about Tiffany?'

'Of course I do.'

'Cass and I loved each other. It makes a difference, Michelle.'

She seemed to wilt before him, and he actually felt genuinely sorry for her. But he hardened his heart against her. She was a good actress. She had played a part to perfection since her accident – the part of a handicapped woman who couldn't manage without him. But this situation – her being pregnant by Aaron Trent – that wasn't the action of a helpless woman, it was a deliberate conniving to get her own way.

'Does Trent know he's going to be a father?' he asked.

'Hell, no.' Her voice was husky. 'I only just found out myself.'

'Are you going to tell him?'

She lifted her shoulders in a painful sort of shrug. 'I don't know. I suppose I should. It wasn't important though – the sex. I don't love him or care about him. How could I? I'd only met him that day. It was exciting in a way – having a man want me again, when I've had nothing but rejection from you for years.'

'Tell me one thing,' he said. 'Just tell me this, Michelle. If I'd agreed to a reconciliation, would you have tried to pass the kid off as mine – even though you knew that Trent was the father?'

'I don't know,' she shrieked, becoming in an instant, hysterical. 'I don't bloody know, Patric. It was just like –

like when you see something in a shop window – a-and you
want it. And you've got the money to pay for it…' Her voice
broke off, she looked away from him, then continued in a
calmer tone, 'I just wanted a baby. And that… that bitch…
you took up with… she's got *your* baby… and I had
nothing… I just wanted to prove that I was capable of doing
the things *she* could do – and at the same time have something for myself as well…'

He went over to her and stood in front of her. 'You feel
no shame about using Trent, do you?' he said.

At last she looked up at him and said, 'No. I feel no
shame. Some men you can do as you like with. Trent
wanted me. He made me feel attractive again, and a whole
woman.'

He looked down into her upturned face with no make up
on it at all at this time of night. She looked old. There were
dark circles beneath her eye and the beginnings of small
lines on her forehead. She looked petulant and stormy – like
a child who's had a favourite toy taken away from it.

'Don't you feel anything for me?' she said, her voice
harsh.

He hesitated, then said, 'I feel – pity. But pity isn't
enough. We can neither of us forget these past two years.'

'Aaron Trent! That bloody man! Flirting with me.
Leading me on.' She began to rail. 'If it hadn't been for
him…'

'You wanted a baby,' he said. 'You went all out to get
what you wanted – as you always have done, Michelle, so
don't go blaming Trent. He's a red-blooded American – and
if you gave him the 'come-on' then, to my mind, you got
all you asked for.'

'So you're not going to challenge him…' Wide eyed she
stared at him.

He laughed harshly. 'What to, Michelle? A duel? Was that one night you spent with him merely to make me jealous? To make me put up a fight for you?'

'I am your wife,' she said, calmer now than she'd been in the past ten minutes.

'You are *not* my wife,' he replied. 'When will you get it into your head that it's over, that the divorce made it quite clear that we were nothing to each other any more.'

'I still think you and I have a future together.' Her face was sullen.

'Michelle…' He knew this conversation would go on all night if he allowed it. What could he do though? How could he convince her their marriage was at an end when she still thought there was hope of a reconcilliation?

She stared at him, open hostility in her eyes now. 'You won't convince me that you and I weren't meant for each other, Patric. I won't let you go. Not ever. You will never – ever – be free of me because I always get what I want in the end.'

She turned away from him at last, and he watched her make her slow and awkward way back to her bedroom. Her shambling, her reliance on the crutches caught at his heart then, because he knew she was a fighter.

After the accident they'd said she would never walk again – but just look at her now. There was dread in his heart though, because he believed the words she'd just spat out at him. He knew that she was a strong woman, and those words of hers had been well thought out and were meant to frighten him into submission.

And he *was* afraid – but not for himself.

It was Cass and the baby who occupied his thoughts now. Michelle, he knew, would stop at nothing to gain her own way. Yes, he was scared.

She turned to look at him as she reached her bedroom door.

'Did I make my meaning clear?' she asked, arching one supercilious eyebrow at him. 'I meant every word – and I *will* have my way.'

He didn't answer. She sickened him.

He heard her soft laughter as she went into the bedroom and, without a sound, closed the door on him.

chapter fifteen

Trent was there as Cass got out of her car at Ashton the following Monday. She'd parked in her usual spot, beside the motorhomes and film trucks.

'Hey – you look peaky,' he greeted her. 'Had a bad weekend or something?'

She hadn't seen Patric on Sunday. He'd phoned her though and told her Michelle was being awkward and he had something to tell her when he saw her again. He'd sounded worried and she wondered if Patric had told Michelle that he knew about Tiffany. She'd asked him if she could do anything to help. He'd told her no, and it was nothing he could discuss over the phone as Michelle was also in the bungalow and could come into the room at any moment.

He'd hung up after saying he'd talk to her the next day at Ashton on the film set, and Cass thought he'd be there to meet her as she parked her car – but he wasn't. She was in no mood for small talk with Aaron Trent however; it was Patric she wanted to see.

She managed a smile in response to Trent's question. 'A *tiring* weekend. I've been scrubbing out the shop – the carpet fitters are coming next week and I had the phone connected the other day. Already people are making bookings for portraits – and I have one wedding – a huge affair by all accounts – waiting to be confirmed this week.'

His brows rose and his good-looking face creased into a smile, 'You really mean business then? It's not just a whim

– opening up that photo place?'

'Trent, I have to make a living.' She faced him as she pushed her car keys into her shoulder bag. 'I won't always have this.' She waved a hand around her. 'I'm just thinking ahead – that's why I decided to buy the place at Rydale Tor.'

'You'll miss us when we've gone.' He laughed.

'Maybe.'

He fell into step beside her as she headed for the nearest motorhome – the one he held the morning meetings in. 'No *maybe* about it, Sandie-baby – you'll have so much time free time on your hands in another few months, you won't know what to do with it.'

'Hardly.' She grimaced. Trent didn't know she had a baby. She liked to keep her private life separate to her working one. Trent thought she lived alone and once her day at the film set was done, her time was her own. Wryly, she thought how wrong he was. Once away from Ashton, Tiff was the only thing in the world that was important to her. Even while she was at Trent's beck and call *at* Ashton, the baby often filled her thoughts. She'd learned though to control those 'mumsy' feelings to some extent when she was working. It wasn't a long day, she told herself. Mostly she was away from here by three at the latest each afternoon. Six hours a day was nothing.

She wished she could convince herself of that fact though! Six hours in reality was plenty of time for Michelle Faulkner to make trouble. But at least she knew that Greer was reliable…

'You and Patric need to sort out this river scene today.' Trent's voice cut into her thoughts, bringing her back to the present, and she realised he was standing waiting for her to precede him into the motorhome. 'Rehearsing it didn't go well last week when you went home with that headache. It needs another run through, and then the real thing. We can't put it off for much longer, babe.'

Patric, to her surprise, was inside the motorhome, talking to Dillon. He looked up and said, 'Hi, Cass – had a good weekend?' And in his eyes and the tone of his voice was a mute apology for not getting away to see her the day before.

'A great Sunday – scrubbing floors,' she replied and sat down at the table opposite him. 'It had to be done though. I'm starting up in business in a fortnight.'

Trent said, 'Sandie is sure trying to make something of that studio – but can we get down to some *real* business?' and he stood, hands on hips looking down on the three of them.

Patric said, 'We're getting there, Trent. Mountains take a bit of a shove to move them though.'

'No, we're not getting there,' Dillon Teasdale fumed. 'I refuse to wear that crap suit you had wardrobe make up for me for one thing. If I'm going to be hurled into the blasted river, I'm doing it in the proper gear – leathers.'

'Look!' Trent shook a finger at him. 'This is none of my doing. You take it up with these two – Sandie and Patric, OK? They were the ones who said it was too dangerous for you to wear leathers.'

'Let me be the judge of that.' Dillon scowled first at Patric then at Cass, before addressing his next remark to her. 'Cass – you know what this will do to me, don't you? With the lads? Can you ever see me living it down if I have to wear that poncy satin suit? What do you take me for? I'll look like Liberace or Elvis in mourning? Or something out of the Sugar-plum-bleeding-fairy ballet?'

She'd never seen Dillon so mad before. 'Hold on,' she said, 'Isn't it better you being in satin than being dragged down under the water?'

'No!' he said. 'I can swim. I'll be OK.'

'You'd need to be a duck to keep afloat in that current,' Cass said.

Patric sighed, leaned back in his seat and said, 'I've been having this argument for the past half hour, Cass. You won't get anywhere pleading with him…'

Trent broke in, 'You have fifteen minutes. No more. Understand?' He turned on his heel and went out of the motorhome, slamming the door so it shook the whole structure.

Cass winced and leaned forward across the table. 'Dillon! Please see reason… Trent's got a lot of money tied up in this.'

'You can talk till you're blue in the face,' Dillon sulked. 'I will not wear that satin. End of argument, Cass.'

She looked at Patric. Patric just shrugged and leaned his head back to gaze up at the roof.

A sudden idea struck her. 'How about a wet-suit? You know, the sort of thing deep sea divers wear? Wouldn't that look like motor-bike leathers on film?'

Dillon groaned. 'Do me a favour, Cass. Wet-suits aren't anything like leathers.'

'On film it wouldn't look too different – and it will be a back view of you they're taking, Dill.' She knew it wasn't an ideal solution, but hoped it might be the compromise they were looking for. When Dillon got into this kind of mood, he was immovable. 'OK,' she said. 'But Trent will probably want to hire a stunt man if you persist in being awkward about this. He's almost at the end of his tether with you.'

'Trent can go and…'

'Dillon!'

He grinned lazily at her. 'I was going to say Trent can go

and jump in the damned river himself,' he said.

Suspiciously she said, 'Yes, I just bet you were going to say that. But think again about that wet-suit, will you?'

Patric slapped a hand down hard on the table. 'I'll go along with that,' he said. 'But you two sort it yourselves, will you? You seem intent on only playing games with each other though, from what I can see of it.'

Cass stared at him. 'What's that remark supposed to mean?'

Patric made an impatient growl in his throat. 'Oh, just forget I spoke,' he said. 'I'm not at my best today.' He got up and said, 'Well, Dillon – what am I to tell Trent? Wet-suit or what?'

Dillon gave a casual shrug. 'So long as I can wear a biker's jacket over it, I suppose it'll do.'

'A jacket's out of the question,' Cass said. 'Leather will hold you down.'

'I'll chuck it off when I hit the water.' Dillon said.

'You'll have enough to do chucking off your boots,' she told him. 'There won't be time for a full scale striptease.'

Patric strode to the door of the motorhome. 'I'll put it to Trent about the wet suit,' he said shortly, 'but be prepared for him to say "No"! He's the one with experience of this sort of thing, and he's also the one who will get the grief if anything untoward happens.'

Dillon grinned. 'Ever had the feeling,' he said, 'that it's going to be one of them days?'

It was all a game to him, Cass realised. It was new and exciting, and nothing like this had ever happened in Dillon's life before. He was being made to feel important, and it was all going to his head.

She got up and raced after Patric, leaving Dillon on his own.

Perhaps if he had nobody to put on an act for, it would do him good. It wasn't like Patric to behave so boorishly as he had done though. Something had obviously upset him.

She caught him up easily; he'd stopped in the middle of the market place against the war memorial and was fumbling in the back pocket of his jeans – she presumed for his mobile phone. Everybody wore jeans who worked on the set. Cass looked down at her own, and the sturdy leather boots that again were part of the 'working gear'.

'What's wrong?' she asked, coming up to him.

'Nothing! Except you and that damned biker being so chummy. I don't like it, Cass.'

'Patric. Don't be like this. You know there's nothing between Dillon and me. You're just taking it too much to heart. Is it so difficult to accept that I've made a place for myself in Derbyshire? Made new friends? Besides, Dillon is a godsend where the studio is concerned. He's done all the electric work needed, re-wiring et cetera, and next week he's giving up his free time to help with the placement of lighting for studio portraits, as well as humping the furniture around.'

He pulled out not his phone, but a crumpled packet of cigarettes and stared down at them in his hand. 'I guess I get carried away with jealousy,' he said. 'Michelle always says I was easier to live with when I smoked twenty a day. Maybe I should go back to the smokes to become a pleasanter person, huh?'

'You've given them up? Altogether?'

He smiled ruefully, 'Yes. Six months ago. This is my 'security blanket' though – this little pack of twenty – still unopened, but battered and bruised from being carried around everywhere with me. D'you think I'm crazy? In need of counselling or something because I get mad every time I see you talking to another man?'

A smile touched her lips. 'I'd think you were more in need of help if you opened that packet and smoked them.'

'I've had a rotten weekend since leaving you and Tiffany, Cass.'

'Me too. I scrubbed and scrubbed at that studio floor – and the phone never stopped ringing – not that I should complain about that, I suppose. It all means business, and if all goes well I'll have my first wedding booked by the end of this week.'

He hardly seemed to be listening to her, she noted.

'Michelle's got something up her sleeve,' he said. 'I can sense it.'

She swallowed. What could she say?

'For one thing, she knows about Tiffany,' he said, crushing his fingers round the cigarette packet till she could see his knuckles turning white. 'I don't know how she knows, but she does.'

She kept silent. He obviously had more to say on the subject.

He shook his head. 'Cass – I've got to talk to you. Can we go somewhere quiet? There have been developments – things you should know about…'

The haunted look in his eyes made Cass feel as if an icy hand had run down the length of her spine. She looked round and saw Trent coming towards them from the direction of the pub. 'Oh, no,' she said. 'Not just now, Patric. You know the mood Trent's in today, and he's haring across the market place towards us right now.'

'But – it's Michelle, Cass – I've got to tell you…'

'Not now. Trent looks real mad…'

'Lunch time, then,' he said. 'Meet me at my car. We'll go and find somewhere where we can get a bite to eat in peace and quiet – away from this lot. It's important, Cass…'

Aaron Trent was breathing heavily as he reached them.

'Just what's going on with you two?' He gazed at each one of them in turn. 'I am *trying* to direct a film! I am *depending* on both of you to help me do that. It seems though that you have more important things to do, so come on – out with it. Let's get this thing out into the open. Sandie-baby, I think you have some explaining to do.'

Patric glared at the man. 'It's none of your damn business.'

'It's my business when the film suffers, man.' Trent was furious.

Cass said quietly, 'He has a right to know, Patric. We have been thinking too much about ourselves, and not enough about the reason we're here – to get this film sorted.'

Patric half turned away.

'No,' she yelled at him. 'That kind of attitude doesn't help, Patric. I think we should come out into the open and tell Trent…'

Patric whirled back to face them both. 'OK,' he said. 'OK – if that's how you want things. Out in the open.'

Without rancour, and without going into unnecessary detail, she told Trent about their affair – and about Tiffany.

He listened in silence, looking stunned when she came to the end of it – which took no more than a minute in all.

'Hell, Sandie, it makes no difference to me about you and Patric but I wish you'd told me about the kid you'd got.'

'I'm sorry I didn't confide in you about Tiffany,' she said.

He held out a hand to her. 'Why the big secret, honey? Lots of girls have babies without being married. And if I'd known about the kid I might have been a bit more adaptable with you. You've put in some pretty weird hours at times here – and I could never understand why you were so eager to rush away in the middle of the afternoons...'

'I'm sorry,' she said again.

'Hell, Sandie, I could have set up a place for you to be with her here. It would have only meant bringing along another lousy caravan as a make-do creche or something.'

'When I knew Patric was going to be involved with the film, I couldn't risk him finding out about her.' She pushed her hands into her jeans pockets and looked at Patric. 'I didn't tell anybody about Tiff. Dillon knew, of course, because he lives in Rydale Tor and he'd been helping me with the electrics and the decorating in the shop I've taken over as a studio.'

'But baby, you didn't know Patric was involved with the film when I first met you,' Trent said, obviously bemused. 'You could have told me about the baby then.'

Cass faced him. 'Trent – you're a man, and you were utterly wrapped up in getting this film sorted. I didn't know if you'd understand. I didn't know how you felt about working mums. You might not have wanted me being so involved if you knew I had other commitments – like a baby, and all a baby entails. And I needed the work – not just for the money, but for the chance to prove to myself that I could cope with a job and a baby...'

'It wouldn't have mattered, Sandie-baby...'

Cass shrugged and carried on, regardless of his interruption. 'There was no reason in the world to tell you I was pregnant,' she said patiently. 'Until Tiff was born, I didn't realise how much time a baby actually took up. I didn't realise either how protective I would feel towards Tiff – how hard it would be to leave her with a nanny every day. It had to be done though. I had something to prove, I suppose – to myself if not to anyone else.'

'All that correspondence we had though.' Trent shook his head, still puzzled. 'All those talks on the phone, Sandie? How on earth did you manage to keep it from me?'

'We never met up in person – not for months if you remember,' she said. 'By the time you and the film crew descended on Derbyshire, I'd already got settled in my flat, had Tiffany, and was a good way through the adaptation. There was no reason at all to tell you I was tied up with a baby – and no husband.'

Still confused, Trent said, 'But Sandie – I wouldn't have expected so much of you if I'd known.'

Patric butted in. 'Cass is stubborn, Trent. Haven't you discovered that for yourself yet? She wouldn't want special treatment. She's proud and she's cussed.'

Warm colour flooded Cass's face. 'You're right in a way, Patric. I didn't want singling out as a special case. I could cope. And I did cope.'

Trent looked from one to the other of them. 'And now what?' he asked, not really meeting Patric's gaze, but concentrating more on her, Cass noted. 'What's with you two?'

'Patric is still tied up with his wife,' Cass said, a stubborn streak making her give Patric a direct and knowing look. 'We have problems. Michelle needs him more than I do, but we're working on it.'

Trent looked down at his feet, rocked backwards and forwards a few times, and still wasn't able to meet Patric's gaze. Cass wondered what had happened between the two men that could make Trent so uneasy in Patric's presence. Trent wasn't usually reticent, or retiring. Trent was usually to the fore in all things, but she sensed an atmosphere between the two of them.

'OK,' he said. 'I guess I know how these things can be.

I'm no saint myself, and I have two ex-Mrs Trents in the States who are draining the cash out of me. I'm human like the rest of the world.'

Patric said, 'So, the interrogation's over, is it Trent?'

Trent finally made eye-contact and said with a shrug, 'Human nature's a funny old thing, Patric. We're none of us saints exactly.'

Patric gave a dry laugh. 'You can say that again.' Then he promptly changed the subject and asked, 'So what's your problem – with this morning's filming, I mean, Aaron?'

Trent seemed – to Cass – to be relieved to be back to a safe subject. 'Danged if I know anything any more,' he said, 'except that we've got to get past this fu….. this river scene. It's holding everything up. We're in the middle of July for God's sake, and I don't want no two-bit prima-donna like Dillon Teasdale holding us up any longer, OK?'

Cass nodded. 'Leave him to me,' she said. 'I'll have another go at him. I have however, suggested that he wears a wet-suit instead of the satin.'

Trent thought about that for a moment then said, 'OK by me, girl, if you think it'll work.'

She glanced at Patric. He said, 'I'll send out for one.'

'Do that,' Trent said. 'Do it now, Patric. Do it yesterday if possible.'

'I need a few words with Cass…'

Trent shook his head. 'Not now. Get that wet suit. It's important.'

'What I want to tell Cass is important.' Patric's jaw was set. He was standing, feet slightly apart, apparently rooted there, with no intention of moving away. 'I need to talk to her right now.'

Trent bawled, 'I need you – "*right now*" – OK? I need you, Patric, to get your ass over them fields and right to that river edge, pronto? OK? Not in ten minutes, not in half-an-hour. Right now! Do you hear me?'

Patric yelled, 'No…'

Cass said, holding up her hands to quieten them both. 'Look, fight this out between yourselves, will you? I made the suggestion – a wet-suit. I can't think of anything else that Dill will agree to. OK? Right?' She looked directly at Patric. 'And I'll meet you at lunchtime. In the car park. And we can talk.'

Patric's lips were set in a thin line of disapproval.

Dillon roared up on the Harley. Trent's side-kick Jefferson bawled out across the square, 'Are we ever goin' to get this show on the bleedin' road?'

Patric was out-numbered. 'OK,' he conceded. 'OK – let's move. Let's forget our private lives for a couple of hours – if we can.' He gave Cass a meaningful look, and as Trent sprang away towards Jefferson, and Dillon sat mutinous on the Harley, revving and revving it, he gave a huge sigh and said, 'Cass – I really do have to talk to you.'

She nodded. 'I'll see you at twelve-thirty. We can't let things get in the way of the filming though.'

Tempers were fraying, she realised. And Dillon wasn't helping, just sitting there revving that bike. She rounded on him as Patric moved to follow Trent.

She yelled at him. 'Dillon – stop that row, will you?'

He did. He killed the engine and whipped off his helmet to yell back, 'Cass – you've got to understand how I feel about this…'

She stormed over to him. 'And you…' she said, breathing hard, 'You, Dillon Teasdale have got to understand that if you don't buckle down and do as you're told – well there are plenty of riders here who can take over that Harley. OK?'

Taken aback, he stared open-mouthed at her. Then he said, 'Cass – I thought you and me were friends.'

'Today,' she said, feeling more like jumping in her car and saying to hell with all of them, 'Today,' she repeated with meaning, 'friends or no friends, you are going to do as I say, Dillon, and that means a wet-suit. *Understand*? A wet-suit – or else I pull out of this little set-up for good.'

chapter sixteen

After they'd all gone, Cass went slowly back to the motorhome. Today hadn't started well. She hoped it would improve before it ended. Until just recently, everything had gone like clockwork. Unfortunately, that damned river scene certainly seemed to have ruffled some tempers and brought out the worst in everybody.

She wasn't looking forward to the afternoon.

As she neared the motorhome they used as a conference office, she heard the sound of a car behind her, and turning her head, saw it going into a parking space between Trent's white limo – that he liked to impress people with – and Patric's dark blue, rather conservative looking car.

She hesitated, one foot on the motorhome step now, one hand on the latch. She didn't recognise the car. If it were some stranger, they might need directions…

She walked away from the motorhome and towards the car. As she neared it, she could see a woman in the driving seat.

She recognised the hair-style – the sleek black hair drawn back from an immaculately made-up face…

'Michelle,' she said, as the woman opened the door and struggled – with the aid of her arm crutches – to get out. 'Can I help?' Cass, though not wanting a confrontation with Michelle, couldn't just stand by and see her having difficulty in manoeuvring herself out of the car.

'No, you Bitch! You've done enough damage in my life. I *can* manage to get myself out of a car,' Michelle tossed back at her.

Cass felt her cheeks burning at the rebuke. 'In that case…' she turned away, embarrassed at Michelle's tone – at the word she had used to her. She didn't want any trouble.

'It's you I've come to see, *bitch*, so don't go stalking off in a paddy,' Michelle called out, and Cass turned round to see that she had managed to get out of the car and was making her way between the parked cars, towards her.

'We'd better go in the motorhome,' Cass said, not wanting Michelle to start up a row – or call her any more names, when just anybody passing might hear.

'No thank you! Can you see me climbing steps in this condition?' Michelle was standing in front of her now, looking absolutely regal in black – long black skirt, black high-waisted jacket that gave the impression she'd been poured into it, black shoes and black leather gloves. The only touch of colour was a scarlet chiffon scarf, fluffed into the neckline of her suit. It didn't look feminine – to Cass it looked positively threatening!

Michelle obviously meant to go no further than the perimeter of the car parking lot. She stood with a hint of defiance in her whole attitude. 'It won't take long,' she said, 'what I have to tell you.'

'To tell me?' Cass was suddenly apprehensive.

'Haven't you seen him yet this morning?'

'Him?' Cass knew only too well who Michelle meant. In some uncanny way though, she knew she had to stall Michelle. She had a feeling that Michelle had come to gloat in some way. Had a feeling too that she herself wasn't going to come out of this meeting at all well.

'Patric, darling girl!' Michelle's tone was pure, vitriolic honey now. 'Patric – my husband, remember? The guy you slept with back in the good old days? The guy who got you pregnant, and whom you're trying your damndest to get your claws into, once again.'

'Michelle – I don't think we have anything to say to each other…' Cass began, but Michelle cut her off with a warning.

'Shut up! Just shut up and listen, will you? It's my turn now.'

Cass clamped her mouth shut.

'He's done it again, girl. Just like he did it with you.'

Cass didn't understand. 'Done what?'

'The pregnant bit. Didn't he tell you? We're having a baby – Patric and me. I just thought I ought to make sure you knew about it, because he, sure as hell, won't broadcast it. He'll keep you hanging on, begging for crumbs of comfort from him. You'll dangle that baby of yours in front of him, and tell him you can't manage without him but you don't stand a chance with him, you know. He's mine. He belongs to me.' Unsteadily, she balanced herself, shoving the crutch in her left hand into her right, peeling off a glove as she did so, and then waving the left hand in front of Cass's nose. 'See this? This is the wedding ring Patric put on my finger more than ten years ago. The divorce – it was all a mistake. He still loves me. That's why I still wear his ring. And this, Bitch, is something you'll never get from your darling Patric because he belongs to me.'

Cass felt all the breath leaving her body, but managed to say in a small trembling voice, 'You're lying – lying about the baby. He would have told me…'

Michelle's face twisted in a cruel smirk of triumph. 'I've *really* got him hooked now, because I too will be able to dangle a baby in front of him and say, 'This is yours' – just as you're doing at the moment. Only I have one big advantage over you. He stays with me. He knows I need him. I just wanted you to be one hundred per cent clear on *that!*'

If Michelle had pulled out a gun and shot her at point-blank range, Cass was sure she couldn't have hit the mark half as well as her words had done. The woman now stood in front of her breathing heavily, but with an expression of elation on her face. And all at once, Patric's words, the words he'd uttered about his marriage two days ago – leapt into her mind. *'I haven't touched her in years'*...and *'There's nothing keeping us together.'*

Then on the phone yesterday, he'd been cagey, saying he had something to tell her and, now – only just now, he'd been insistent he should talk to her because he had something of importance to tell her.

Well! Now she knew, didn't she? And she felt like she'd been taken for a ride all along by Patric. She felt humiliated and hurt – and angry.

She stared hard at Michelle and stammered out, 'You...you're lying. You're just trying to...' she threw up her hands despairingly, 'trying to hurt me...'

Michelle's smile was pure evil. 'My baby's due around February next year. You can count on your fingers what that means, can't you, my dear? It means that while we've been here – in Derbyshire – in our cosy little bungalow on the moors, Patric and I have reached a new understanding – it means, to be crude – *bitch* – that he and I have been "at it like rabbits" – if you get my meaning?'

Cass waited to hear no more. She set off at a run to her own car, parked a little way away, delved into the pocket of her jeans for her keys, and literally threw herself into the driving seat.

She tried not to look at Michelle as she reversed out of the parking lot, but the presence of the woman was there in her rear view mirror, in her side-wing mirrors, and through the windows as she twisted round to get the car out into the open – and quick!

When the car was pointing in the 'out' direction, she could see Michelle in front of her, that smile still on her face, a smug, self-satisfied, evil smile now. She was standing there, with her crutches supporting her – and it would be so easy to…

Cass quickly revved the engine. Somehow she must try and get past Michelle. There was a wide open space all the way round the woman, but helpless as she was, and unable to run or leap out of the way, Michelle was a sitting target.

It made no difference. As much as she hated Michelle, Cass knew there was no way she was capable of deliberately hurting her. Doing that would make her no better than Michelle, herself. It would put her in the same position Michelle had been in when she'd run her car at her own lover some eighteen months ago now. She could in some way, however, understand what Michelle had been feeling when she'd killed Craig Andrews, because the same feelings were running in and out of Cass's mind right now. In these last few minutes, her world had fallen apart. It had become obvious to her that Patric had betrayed her. Despite all he'd said about Michelle in the past, he obviously still found her attractive. And he'd lied to her. Cass couldn't take that. She knew she'd never trust him again because he'd lied!

She sped away, giving Michelle a wide berth, and seeing in her rear view mirror Michelle making her way back to her car. Once out of the car park, she headed up onto the high Derbyshire moorland, not knowing where she was going or what she was going to do.

Only one thing was certain in her mind now. And that

was the fact that she never, *ever* wanted to see Patric Faulkner again – as long as she lived.

She'd calmed down by the time she got back to Rydale Tor, and was thinking more logically as she let herself into the flat.

Upstairs, Cass found Greer feeding Tiffany mashed-up vegetable, and there was a little baked custard on the table for her pudding. Tiff was in her high chair, and Cass said, 'Hi, Greer,' and then went over to the baby and kissed her on the top of her head.

Tiff banged her little fists on her table and opened her mouth for more food. Greer laughed softly and carried on feeding the baby, apparently sensing there was something wrong to bring Cass back to the flat so early in the day, but not wanting to cause an atmosphere by asking questions. She said, 'Your daughter's like a little bird, not a bit fussy about food – eats everything put in front of her.' She glanced at Cass. 'Hey – make yourself a coffee or something. You look awful.'

Cass put the kettle on, then moved over to the window while Tiffany finished her lunch. She stood there with her back to both baby and Greer, until she heard Greer saying, 'Good girl! Not a bit of pudding left.'

She turned around and went to make herself that coffee. As she poured the strong liquid into a cup, Cass became aware that Greer was standing beside her, rinsing out Tiffany's lunchtime dishes.

'Something wrong?' Greer gave her a meaningful look, while behind them both, Tiffany sang and cooed and banged with a plastic spoon on her high-chair table.

Cass didn't feel in the mood for another confrontation. She just shook her head, unable to speak, picked up her coffee and went and sank down on the sofa.

Greer busied herself with Tiffany, putting the little girl down in her play-pen, giving her some soft toys and large plastic building cups to occupy her.

There was a radio-cassette player on a wooden sewing box beside the play-pen, and Greer chose a cassette and started playing it quietly near the baby. Tiffany rocked and jigged and banged the plastic cups about to a Disney selection of tunes.

Greer went and sat beside Cass. 'You've got some colour back in your face,' she stated. 'You looked absolutely awful when you came in. Want to talk about it?'

The phone started ringing before Cass could answer. Greer reached for it but Cass said, 'No – leave it. I don't want to talk to anybody.'

They both sat holding their breath and staring at each other until it stopped ringing, then Greer said, 'I hope it wasn't something important.'

Cass said, 'I don't think so.' Then the mobile in her bag set up an insistent bleeping, and Greer looked at her in some concern. 'Aren't you going to answer it?'

'No.'

'Are you going back to work this afternoon.'

'No.'

'But…'

Cass got up from the sofa. 'I feel like packing my bags, and going as far away as possible from Rydale Tor, and telling Aaron Trent he can stuff his film.'

'Problems on the set?'

'Problems, full stop. Not just on the set.' Cass pulled a wry face. 'Is anything ever achieved by running away though?' she asked Greer, then answered her own question by saying, 'No, of course it isn't. I'm big enough, old enough, and fool enough to know that problems don't resolve themselves.'

'You want to run away?' Greer stared at her, wide-eyed.

'I would love to run away,' Cass said drily.

'You could take a holiday, I suppose…'

'A holiday?' Cass laughed without any mirth in the sound. 'A holiday would be running away, Greer. Like I ran away from Suffolk eighteen months ago. The only trouble with running away is that at some time you've got to face up to your problems – and often run back home.'

'But this is your home now…'

'Yes,' Cass said quietly. 'This is my home and I'm through with running away. I'm staying here. I'm going to see this damn film through to the end, and then I am going to get my life in order – and keep it in order.'

'Good for you,' Greer said, also getting up from the sofa and going over to look at Tiff in the play-pen.

'The only thing is,' Cass said with a wry smile, 'I am not going to answer that phone until I'm in a better temper than I am now. OK?'

Greer looked at her from across the room. 'You're the boss, Cass. I'm just paid to do as I'm told. I do, however, think you've been working too hard just lately – and far be it from me to preach, but I think a bit of a holiday wouldn't go amiss for you and Tiff. And for what it's worth – I wouldn't class that as 'running away' – would you?'

'Maybe we could do with a little holiday. I can't really get away this week though. It's a crucial point of the film – and, of course, next week I'm going to be doubly busy – with Aaron Trent and his tantrums, and also with the pre-opening days of the studio downstairs. By the way,' she hesitated, 'have those people phoned about the wedding? They did say they'd give me a definite booking this week and so far…' she shrugged, 'I did leave the answer-phone on downstairs, but…'

'I did hear it ringing this morning,' Greer said. 'But as I don't have a key to the studio…'

'Oh, heck. I forgot to tell you – there's one hanging in the key cupboard in the kitchen.' Cass sighed. The wedding she'd been promised was important. It was a big affair for Rydale Tor – a well-known local businessman's daughter. It was a big chance for Cass to show what she could do too. She really needed that booking, and she could have kicked herself for not leaving – or even giving – Greer a key to the downstairs studio.

'Want me to go and check?' Greer was half-way to the kitchen already.

'Would you, Greer. I feel absolutely whacked, and I've got an idea about that break you said I needed.'

When Greer came back upstairs it was to tell Cass that the caller hadn't left a message.

'Damn!'

Greer went and hung the key up again, then came back out of the kitchen and said, I've put the kettle on – you've let your coffee go cold, so I'm making some more. Just sit down and put your feet up will you?'

'About that break…'

'Forget it, Cass. I was speaking out of turn. I know how busy you are.'

'And how worried over this Patric business. His wife came to see me this morning, you see…'

'Ah! I see now why you don't want to answer the phone.'

'I can't bring myself to speak to her again.'

'And you think it was her?'

Cass shrugged. 'It could have been Patric, but I think if I speak to Patric just at this moment, I shall say things I'll regret for the rest of my life, so…' She shrugged again. 'The only trouble is, he'll probably come here.'

'And you don't want to see him?'

'I think perhaps he won't want to see me – but he will want to see Tiff.'

Greer nodded. 'It's only natural, I suppose.'

'So – I've been thinking…'

Greer looked interested.

'Why don't you and Tiff go away for a few days. It will give me time to sort myself out, and to let Patric know that there's no point in him coming over here for a while.'

'You'd trust me to take Tiff off somewhere?'

Cass laughed softly. 'Of course I'd trust you. I trust you with her every day, don't I?'

'We-ell, yes…'

'So what do you say to a really nice hotel – somewhere not too far away, but somewhere you can have everything done for you – meals got ready, beds made, and perhaps a view of the sea from your window?'

Greer was quiet for a moment or two. She seemed to be mulling things over in her mind as she went into the kitchen again and came out with two mugs of coffee. She sat down beside Cass then and they both looked across at Tiff, who had fallen asleep in her play-pen, cuddled up to a soft, fluffy-teddy-bear.

'I don't want to sound ungrateful,' Greer said. 'But I'm not sure about the sea-side at this time of year? It'll be hectic on the beaches. I like the idea of giving you a bit of time – and space – to yourself though, so what about if I took Tiff home with me for a few days.'

'Home! Rydale Tor!' Cass pulled a face. 'Hardly a holiday, or even a break.'

'She'd be near to you if she didn't settle though.' Greer

looked thoughtful. 'You never know with kiddies, do you? And you're going to miss her anyway, and if she's near – only a couple of miles away – but actually on your doorstep, well…'

'It's an idea. Would your mother mind though?'

'She'd love having Tiff there. Oh, Cass, let me take her. You can tell Patric in all honesty then that I've taken Tiffany away for a few days, and it will be the truth. It will keep him out of your hair for a while.'

'When Tiff wakes up, then?' It seemed a perfect solution to Cass. It would mean she could concentrate wholly on the film while she was at Ashton each day, and she could finish off the downstairs studio in her spare time. She knew too, that if she kept busy, she wouldn't be able to fill her mind with the thought of Patric and Michelle – together again – and expecting their first baby.

'I'll go and pack a few of Tiff's things, shall I?' Greer stood up again.

Cass nodded. 'Could you put them in the car – and then you'd better go and prepare your mum for what's about to descend on her, OK?'

'I could take Tiff in her buggy.'

'No – you get off home, Greer, and I'll bring her over around tea-time this afternoon. It's no more than five minutes in the car to your home.'

'OK!' Greer was full of enthusiasm. She paused at the door. 'Do you know – I'm really going to enjoy this.'

chapter seventeen

Patric couldn't think why Cass was nowhere around at lunchtime – especially when he'd asked her to meet him in the car park, and she'd known he so desperately needed to talk to her.

He rang her home number and there was no reply. He rang her mobile – and likewise – no response.

He checked the motorhome, then walked to the pub. She wasn't there and no one could remember seeing her since early that morning. Going back to the car park, he discovered her car wasn't there, and he began to worry that perhaps something had happened to Tiffany, and that the girl who looked after her had phoned Cass to go home.

He tried ringing her number at the flat again, but still there was no reply.

Thoughts of Michelle sprang to mind; was she out there causing trouble? He was edgy and jittery and missed lunch altogether, walking around asking people – bikers, Dillon, anybody and everybody if they'd seen Cass, or if she'd said where she was going.

Nobody had seen her. Nobody knew anything, it seemed.

Aaron Trent came into the pub while he was there for the second time. Trent slumped onto a high stool against the bar and said, 'Have you guys seen what's happening out there? It's raining. Coming down in buckets – as these folk in Derbyshire say. Me – I'd say it was more like a Texas gusher. But what the hell! We shan't get that river scene done today – especially as we still haven't got that wet-suit for Teasdale, so I'm calling it a day – OK? I'm getting in my car and driving straight back to my hotel – and do you know what? – I'm going to sit in that damned bar when I get there – and drown my sorrows!'

Aaron Trent walked into his hotel foyer, walked half-way across the wide, carpeted floor before he sensed he was being watched. He stopped, hairs prickling at the back of his neck, then swiftly turned around to look at the comfortable seating area up against the windows, which provided panoramic views over Derbyshire.

'What the…'

She never moved. She just sat there, looking at him like a Black Widow Spider, he thought. Or, maybe with that red thing round her neck, like an Ozzie red-back – deadly, calculating, and watching him like she was going to eat him up.

He walked over to her. 'Mrs Faulkner. What a surprise.'

Her face was pale – white almost. The crutches were leaning up against the seat next to her. There was nobody else about. It was mid-afternoon – why should there be anyone else around? She'd probably scared them all away, sitting there looking as though she was some avenging angel.

'You're early. And don't come all polite on me,' she said, breathing shallowly. 'And after what happened between us a few weeks ago, I wouldn't think calling me 'Mrs' the most appropriate or tactful way of going about things, would you?'

'Michelle, honey…'

'Aaron, *honey*,' she mocked, and managed a smile of sorts. But it just sort of pulled at her lips and made them look mean – and even more hungry than the red-back.

'We had to abandon filming. The rain…' He hunched his shoulders, 'That and Teasdale's bloody-mindedness anyway, and your husband's surliness. What's wrong with folks today anyhow? Sandie walks out on me as well – so what the hell. I came back here.' He tilted his head back, looked up at the ceiling and shoved his hands on his hips. 'And I mean, what the hell! I've had it with them. I told them – get it sorted – everything – the tantrums, the private lives, the whole caboodle. Get it sorted. Because bright and early tomorrow morning, we're doing that river scene – and we're going to do it *my* way.'

'Isn't that how you always do things,' Michelle asked archly. 'Your way, Aaron?'

'No, sweetie, it isn't. I'm a sucker. I get taken in by folks because I'm a real nice guy and I like things to be plain sailing. I don't ask for a great deal. I do ask for consideration though in my working life.'

She looked up at him. 'It's what I ask for too,' she said. 'Consideration. It seems beyond the bounds of some people though. They just take what they want, then they drop you. Haven't you found that so, Mister Trent?'

'Hey! If you're aiming to say something, then why not just say it, plain and simple-like?'

'You haven't tried to get in touch with me – not for weeks, not since…'

'Yeah! Yeah!' Aaron flapped his hands. 'I've been one busy guy though. You know how it is, Michelle – right?'

'Too busy for another roll in the hay?'

'Hey – Michelle, it was good. But it was, as they say, a one-off, wasn't it? We both needed a bit of company that night a couple of weeks ago.'

'Over a month ago,' she said. 'How time flies when you're having fun! And I just bet you've been having plenty of that – haven't you, Mister Trent?'

'A couple of weeks, a month, six months..? What does it matter? I do things on impulse, Michelle honey. I don't need no diary.'

'But I do,' she said. 'And my diary is what tells me that neither of us took precautions that night, more than a month ago.'

'It wasn't exactly something we planned though, was it, Michelle?' He had dropped down on to the seat the other side of her now and was leaning forward, his voice lowered, despite there being no one else in the room with them.

'The night – or the baby?' she asked.

He just stared at her. Then he said, 'A baby? You've got to be joking.' And he was glad he'd decided to sit down because all of a sudden he felt real weak – especially around the knees.

'I don't joke about important things. There's going to be a baby – and I'm not joking, believe me.'

'But there's Patric? Why come to me?' He spread his hands out wide in front of him. 'It could be Patric's – he is, after all, your husband?'

'I haven't slept with Patric for over two years. I haven't slept with anyone in those two years – except you.'

He stared at her, and swallowed painfully. Then he drawled, 'O'mi'Ga-ad!'   'And Patric knows.'

'Oh, no!' He sat shaking his blonde unruly head from side-to-side, saying, 'No, no, no…!'

She said in a practical voice, 'I want to keep it. The baby.'

He changed from shaking to nodding his head now. 'Yeah! Yeah! Anything you want, honey, athough wouldn't it be best if… well, if we got you in some private clinic. I'd pay of course…'

'I want the baby.' It was said with a finality that stunned

him. When she followed it up with, 'Will you marry me?' Aaron felt as if she'd put a loaded shot-gun to his head, and had a parson waiting by in the bar!

'I have a wife in the States, honey,' he told her quickly. 'Actually, I have *three* wives in the States to be exact. One permanent for the time being, and the other two costing me a packet in alimony. The permanent one is very "understanding" if you get my meaning. Not clingy like some women. Not since I settled a million dollar deal on her. A little "arrangement" that keeps her happy – and outa my hair.'

'But…'

'I'm just telling you this, honey,' he interjected quickly, 'Because I don't want you to run away with the idea that you can turn any tables – or make any threats – such as trying to blackmail me. OK?'

She doubled up, right there in front of him! Doubled up, gasping and clutching at her stomach. He shot out of his chair yelling, '*Hey*! You all right?'

She straightened, fell back with her head against the soft leather of the chair. She was whiter than white now and had bit on her lip till it was bleeding, a thin trickle of blood running onto her chin.

He knelt in front of her and one of her hands grabbed at his. Her fingernails bit into the skin of his wrist making him wince. He tried to disengage her hand with his free one prising away at her fingers, but she wouldn't let go.

He was getting scared. 'What is it, honey?'

'I don't know. It's been like this on and off the last week.' At last her fingers loosened from his wrist. 'I guess it's early pregnancy – I suppose it can get you like this. I have been sick a couple of times.'

'You don't get pain though – not this early. I got five kids back in the States and I was there right through from conception to when they were born. There's pain then – and there's pain after – 'specially when they all get to high school and want Pa to buy them automobiles, but…'

She doubled up again and when the pain had passed, she said weakly, 'I hope it's not like this for the whole nine months.'

'You should see a doctor. Have you got a good MD? Let me call him…' He jumped to his feet, swiftly turning away in the direction of the reception area.

'No!' She stopped him by calling out, 'Look – I'm OK now. It's passed. It's probably because I'm so tense about this whole thing.'

He gave her his full attention. 'Let me drive you back home.'

She shook her head. 'It's not necessary. I have my own car outside.'

'You said Patric knew… about you and me. Does he know about the kid?'

'Yes.'

He crouched in front of her. 'And?'

'He doesn't care what happens to me.'

He shook his head, and patted her hand. 'I don't believe that. He's a real good guy.'

She shrugged. 'Believe what you like. You don't know Patric as well as I do though. Just help me to my feet will you? These seats are so low down they're cramping me up.'

He got her to standing position and handed her the crutches. 'I'll see you out to your car. You are OK to drive back to the bungalow, I take it?'

She didn't tell him that the car was stacked with all her things from the bungalow up on the moors. She didn't tell him she wasn't going to return there – ever. She didn't know yet where she was going. She supposed she could always go home to Suffolk. She'd have to pass through Rydale Tor if she did that. And something kept drawing her back there. It had become a kind of mini-obsession with her – driving into the little town and parking her car, then walking as best she could along the promenade by the side of the river.

She never went farther than Cass Fairburn's flat though. Somehow she managed to walk that far and no further. It was then that she sat down on the seat beside the river, and watched the flat – and the shop underneath it that was having work done on it. The other day a man had come and stencilled 'Cassandra' right across the window. When she went again, the letters had been filled in with black. It fascinated her – watching Cass's flat – and the shop.

'Phone me. If you need me. Phone me.' Aaron Trent looked deep into her eyes.

She gave him stare for stare. 'I will – if I need you. I don't somehow think I shall need you though.'

'The money…'

'I don't need your money. I've got money of my own. It doesn't do any good though, does it. Not when you've got insurmountable problems.'

'Nothin's insurmountable, Michelle.' He was seeing a different side to her, she realised – a woman who had maybe left it too late for the important things in life and was now clutching at straws.

She still looked at him steadily and said, 'Oh, yes. Some things are. Some things are meant to be – and I've got a feeling that one of those things is about to take me over.'

'Baby – you're scaring me silly talking like that. You will let me know…'

'No, Aaron,' she replied. 'It's not your problem any

more.' She leaned forward, kissed him gently full on the lips, and then started making her slow and ponderous way across to the hotel's wide doors.

chapter eighteen

Patric drove home around three o'clock and noticed that Michelle's car was not at the bungalow. Inside, the woman he'd hired to clean the place was just finishing off the chores.

'Did my wife say where she was going?' Patric asked.

'No, Mr Faulkner. She was all ready to leave when I turned up at lunchtime. She'd tidied up her bedroom – told me I didn't need to go in there today.'

'Michelle – tidied up?'

The woman smiled. 'Yes. I peeped in and was surprised – there's not even a powder compact been left out – everything's ship-shape. Even the bed was made.'

Patric set off at a run down the hall and pushed open the door to Michelle's bedroom. He stood there and gazed around. Michelle had never been a tidy-bedroom type of woman. This bedroom un-nerved him. There wasn't a thing out of place.

He went over to the run of wardrobes built along one wall, and slid the doors open one-by-one. Not a thing of hers was left inside – not a dress, a slip, or a shoe. The wardrobes had been completely cleared out.

He pulled drawers open in the dressing table. They were empty. He sought in the bathroom for signs of Michelle – expensive bath essences, her toothbrush, her make-up, body sprays – but they were all gone.

He went over to the bedside telephone and dialled her mobile number, but her phone was switched off.

His stomach started churning. This was weird. First Cass's phones not being answered – and now Michelle's! Could the two be connected? Had Michelle gone looking for Cass? And if so…

He didn't dare start surmising why Michelle should want to contact Cass. He took a last look round the room, then closed his eyes and said hoarsely to himself, 'Why? What's behind all this?'

He went through each room, looking for a note propped up against a clock, or on a bedside table or in the kitchen by the toaster. When he realised she had left nothing in the way of telling him where she had gone, he went outside again and checked the garage.

It was empty. The whole place was empty of Michelle's presence. It was as if she'd never existed.

The phone in the hall started ringing as he came out of the garage, and he raced back inside the bungalow and snatched it up.

It was Aaron Trent.

'It's Michelle,' Trent said shortly. 'She was here Patric.'

'Here? Where the hell is 'here'?'

'At my hotel.'

'Doing what,' Patric snapped.

'Just wanted to talk to me. I was worried though. She didn't seem at all well. At one point she was doubled up in pain. She left me around an hour ago – but gave me no clue as to where she might be going. I didn't know whether to call you or not. She was in a pretty strange mood, see, and…'

'Where did she go? Do you know? Did she give you any clue…?'

'It's anybody's guess, man. She just went.'

'But where to? She certainly hasn't returned here.' Patric

was becoming exasperated.

'I told ya! I just don't know where she is now. I thought you should know – that there's something not quite right with her. She nearly passed out on me. I tell you, man, she was in some sort of pain. And usually she seems so tough, Patric – so able to take care of herself. You know she's tough. I just thought you should know though that she came here – but you know what – now she's gone, I've got the craziest feeling. It's like she was never here, man. Never existed. I tell you – it's just plain crazy.'

Patric knew the feeling. It was something he couldn't put into words though. It was as if Michelle had been magically spirited away and out of their lives. He put the phone down after saying he'd check her friends and see if she'd contacted any of them. But as he did so he felt prickles of apprehension down his spine, almost as if he'd just been shut into an ice box.

He shook himself and tried to rid his mind of the thought of that night two years ago when the police had arrived at the house in Suffolk to tell him about Michelle's accident. He closed his eyes, reliving that night – and wondering why it had come back to haunt him on a brilliant July afternoon, when the sun was shining after a downpour of torrential rain.

To distract himself, he called some of her friends. She didn't have many though. And those she did look on as her closest acquaintances all lived in Suffolk, where she'd been born and lived for all of her life. When none of these so-called friends could throw any light on where she might be, he dialled Michelle's mobile number again but it was still switched off.

He tried Cass's number again and there was no reply.

For one frantic moment he thought about calling the

police, but realised that both Michelle and Cass were grown women. He couldn't report them missing – as if they were children gone off the rails. And the police certainly wouldn't be interested in the domestic side of their quarrels and disputes.

He paced up and down the hall. His mind seemed to have gone blank on him. He couldn't think what to do next. His first impulse was to rush over to Rydale Tor and hammer on Cass's door. He reasoned though that if she were there she would have answered her telephone.

He went down the passage to the kitchen. The cleaning woman had just made a pot of tea.

She smiled at him. 'I thought you looked as if you needed something strong.'

How right she was, he thought as his fingers curled round the battered old packet of cigarettes in his pocket. But he didn't take them out. If he had done, he knew he would have lit one up.

Michelle was drawn back to Rydale Tor. She drove through the little town which was filled with holiday-makers at this time of year. The shops were crowded, the pavements and promenade spilling over with people now the rain had stopped. The bikers who were such a feature of the place, were out in force, roaring through the main street, or else milling around the lined-up bikes which were parked diagonally, at the side of the road in several different places.

Leather-clad bikers lounged around and leaned upon their gleaming ton-up machines – those machines which were lavished with love and cared for as tenderly as any human baby could yearn for. Some of the crowd – all ages and both sexes – munched on hot doughnuts, bags of chips, and hot dogs and hamburgers from the stalls across the road on the river-bank, ignoring the smart cafés and restaurants that the less flamboyant tourists frequented.

There were climbers on the face of the Tor – that great sheet of solid rock that gave the place its name. And above them, the cable cars carried sight-seers from the top of the Tor to the other hills on the opposite side of the road, while the little valley below hustled and bustled with life, holiday-makers, and traffic.

Michelle parked easily because she could ignore yellow lines on the road and ''no-parking zones' with her disability-scheme car badge. She parked on the same side of the road as, and as near as she could to Cass Fairburn's flat – and the shop beneath it. She didn't care really whether Cass saw her or not.

She sat looking out through her half-opened side window. She didn't know why she'd come here. She felt ill. She felt sick. And that pain – it kept coming back – a griping sensation in her side that built up and up and had her sweating and biting hard on her lips to stop herself crying out.

She'd read up about miscarriages. She didn't want to lose the baby though. She was determined to carry it to full-term. If Cass Fairburn could carry a child for nine months, so could she. She had never given in to anything in her whole life and she wasn't going to let a bit of pain get her down. She wanted this baby. She had to prove that she was as good as Cass – could achieve the same thing as Cass had done in bearing a child.

She wasn't concerned overmuch about its father. That part of the equation didn't matter to her. It was personal achievement that mattered – and a child would be an experience if nothing else, she decided. It would be fun having a small life to mould exactly as she wanted to mould it. And if she got fed up with it – well, there were always nannies you could employ…

Aaron Trent's baby though – now that was something else altogether. Perhaps she'd be able to give an interview to some magazine or newspaper when it was born… a pretty blonde-headed caricature of the man himself.

How long she sat there daydreaming, she didn't know, but the pain had subsided now to a dull thumping ache. There had been no bleeding, so perhaps it wasn't the start of a miscarriage. Perhaps if she thought positively about producing a living, breathing, full-term child, it would all turn out all right.

It was hot in the car. She craved some fresh air. Outside, on the river bank, the leaves on the trees were fluttering in the cool air rising from the water. She pushed open the car door, and with the aid of her crutches managed to get out. Day by day, it was getting easier to manoeuvre herself around. Inside the bungalow, she'd been able to manage with just one crutch – and it had been a delight to her to be able to carry a teapot to the table, or balance a plate of sand-wiches in her free hand.

She tested her weight out in the open – and muttered a triumphant '*Yes!*' before leaning inside the car again and tossing one crutch on to the back seat.

Nobody took any notice of a woman walking along slowly with one crutch. There were so many people about that one more made no difference. There were bikers in leathers, there were children with ice-creams, there were wheel-chairs and buggies, and men in shorts and women with shopping bags, all nudging shoulders, meandering from shop to shop, traipsing across the road to look at the ducks or buying picture postcards, and standing in groups at bleeping traffic lights…

Michelle hesitated in front of the whitewashed window of Cass Fairburn's studio. It had '*Cassandra*' written in large black script across the outside, and there was gold shading on the letters now. In smaller print was the word '*Photographer*' – and Michelle's lips curled in a sneer – even the name '*Cassandra*' seemed to be mocking her, telling her that this *Cassandra* had everything while she, *Michelle*, had nothing of great value in her life any more.

She was still standing outside the whitewashed, blanked-out window, when she heard the side door being unlocked. She decided to stay put. If Cass and the baby came out – well, she'd as much right as anyone else to be in Rydale Tor, Michelle told herself. There was no law against standing outside the shop belonging to her rival – her one-time husband's lover.

She almost laughed out loud, and she wondered if Patric had managed to placate Cass yet and convince her that he wasn't, in fact, the father of the child his ex-wife was carrying inside her.

As the door opened slightly, she could hear Cass talking to the child.

'Ups-a-daisy now. Your little car-seat is awkward in a tiny little space like this doorway.'

She heard the child chuckling and cooing, saw a little arm waving a pale-pink teddy-bear around and then dropping it just outside the doorway.

Cass put the car-seat down on the ground inside the doorway, and leaned part way out of the doorway to pick it up and give it back to Tiffany. If Cass had turned her head at that moment, Michelle knew she couldn't have helped but see her. Cass's attention however was on the child.

And then, from inside the shop, a phone started to ring.

Cass seemed flustered. She began sorting through a

bunch of keys and saying to Tiffany, 'Mummy must get to the phone, love. It's bound to be that big wedding booking which I've been expecting. I'll have my eye on you all the time though. Just be a good girl and sit still…

Michelle heard the lock click and Cass's footsteps echoing across a tiled floor. She heard her calling back to the child, 'Only one minute, precious. Mummy will be back in just a minute…'

Michelle edged to the doorway and peeped round it. The baby was happily playing with the pink teddy as she sat strapped into her small car-seat. Cass was inside the studio talking on the phone, only a few feet away from the child. Michelle heard her saying, 'Just hang on a couple of seconds, please…I've mislaid my pen and diary…I remember, they're in the bottom drawer…I need to find my desk keys…'

With Cass flustered and preoccupied – it was so easy for Michelle to scoop up the car-seat and melt into the crowd. She couldn't believe it had been so easy.

Within seconds she heard Cass screaming, '*My baby – my baby*…!' But, by then, Michelle was opening her car door, sliding in behind the wheel and placing the baby on the front passenger seat, before quickly looping the safety belt around the child's seat and swiftly starting up the engine.

There was no need to hurry. She was just another driver pulling out into the stream of traffic that was Rydale Tor in the height of summer. Her tinted windows would keep prying eyes away from Tiffany – and there hadn't been time for Cass to both raise the alarm and give a description of the baby.

It was three miles further on that the first police car, siren screaming, passed her on the opposite side of the road, heading for Rydale Tor. It was closely followed by two more.

Michelle allowed herself a little laugh of triumph.

They wouldn't catch her now. She'd be well away by the time they'd taken statements and asked for witnesses to come forward.

She looked down at the baby at her side. Tiffany beamed at her and jigged up and down in her little seat.

Michelle marvelled at the tiny fingers twirling pink teddy round and round, felt a sense of triumph too as Tiffany's dark, dark eyes, so like the eyes of her daddy, gazed at her with trust. She convinced herself in that moment that it was right for the child to be with her. Tiffany, so dark and pretty, resembled both her and Patric, she decided, much more so than Cass with her fair hair and skin.

It had been so easy. She'd been in the right place at the right time. And what was happening now made up for all the heartache Patric had put her through.

'Ireland,' Michelle said solemnly to the baby. 'Yes. That's where I'll take you, baby. That's where I'll have that little sister or brother for you too. We'll be safe there. There's a place – a place that not even my darling Patric knows about, where we'll be safe. And nobody will ever even guess where we are…'

chapter nineteen

Michelle drove for half an hour, before pulling into a lay-
by just as she was leaving Derbyshire and heading north
for the M6 motorway that would take her to Liverpool.
Taking out her phone she dialled Patric's mobile.

She guessed by now he'd be at Rydale Tor – comforting
Cass, or maybe berating her for not taking more care of
Tiffany. She knew that, without question, the police would
be involved.

He answered straightaway, and when she replied he
snapped out, 'Where are you, for God's sake? What are you
up to now?'

She took a deep breath, made her voice perfectly normal.
'Darling – I've just looked in my handbag and discovered
the note I intended leaving for you. I was feeling decidedly
under the weather and thought it best if I came home to
Suffolk. I must have popped the note into my bag instead
of leaving it on the coffee table for you.'

'You're in Suffolk? Now?'

'Well nearly,' she lied. 'Not quite home, but near enough.
Another hour and I will be. I thought if I were back early
enough I'd call in on Doctor Abbott and make an appointment for a check-up.'

She smiled grimly to herself. If Patric believed her – that
she was indeed nearly home, no one on earth would suspect
she had Tiffany with her because she couldn't have covered
such a vast distance since the baby had been snatched. At
all costs, she had to keep the knowledge to herself that she

was driving North West, not South East. Nobody must have the slightest inkling that she was making her way to Liverpool where she could get a ferry across to Ireland.

At the moment, little Tiff was fast asleep in the baby seat beside her but Patric, she could tell, was suspicious.

'Where are you?' he demanded grimly, and she had the feeling that somebody else was with him, listening in on the conversation.

'Heading towards Thetford, darling. Do you remember the little shop where you used to pull up to buy cigarettes? I needed a drink, but all they had were those little boxes of fruit juice that you drink through a straw so I'm making do with that and it's not at all bad really – apple juice – quite refreshing…'

Keep it cool, she told herself, keep it mundane. Above all – keep it ordinary and believable.

'Michelle!' She heard him give a heavy sigh. 'Michelle – shut up for a minute, will you?'

'What is it, darling?' She kept an eye on Tiffany who was stirring in her sleep. It wouldn't do for the baby to wake up and start crying.

'Michelle, there's some trouble here. It's Tiffany – Cass's baby…' He corrected himself almost immediately by saying, 'Our baby. She's gone missing – and Michelle…'

There was a muffled noise now coming over the phone – as if someone were whispering something.

Instantly she cried, 'Patric – oh, darling, how awful! When…? How…? Look – do you want me to come back in case I can help in any way?'

'No. No…Michelle – you don't know anything about this, do you…?'

She forced a tremor to her voice. '*Me*! 'Me, Patric? What on earth do you mean? How could *I* know anything…?'

'I'm sorry, Michelle. I had to ask. But…'

'Have you informed the police? Are they there?'

'Yes. Yes, of course we have. There are people out searching the riverbank –the river itself…' His voice broke off on the sound of a sob. There was a strangled pause before he continued, 'Look – this is serious. There's a Detective Chief Inspector here…'

She made her voice harsh. 'Well, let me speak to him, will you, Patric? Maybe *he* won't make accusations against me over the phone, like you seem to be doing!'

'Michelle, I am not judging you. I am worried out of my head though. We all are…'

'It sounded remarkably like an accusation to me.'

'Just give me exact details of where you are…the police…they can't rule anything out at the moment…'

'Patric – how long has the child been missing?'

'About half-an-hour…'

'And how long do you suppose it would have taken me to get to Thetford?'

'Michelle…please…'

'Three-and-a-half hours at least, Patric. You know damn well…'

'*OK* ! *OK* !'

There were more muffled sounds on the phone. Beside her, Tiffany was stretching and yawning.

Patric came back on the phone. 'Are you on the motorway?' he asked.

She gave a gentle laugh. 'Patric – why don't you just put the policeman on the phone to me? I can tell there's some-body there telling you what to say, because you know as well as I do that there are no motorways leading to this part of Suffolk.'

There was a pause. Then another voice. A woman's. 'DCI

Erin Scholes, here, Mrs Faulkner. We just need to know your exact whereabouts. Which roads you've been on. Which road you're on now.'

'You're checking on me?' Michelle felt her heart give a lurch, and that damned pain started up again.

'We're checking all possibilities.'

'*OK* – I'm on the...'

'Let's start from the beginning, shall we? What time did you leave Derbyshire?'

Michelle closed her eyes against the pain, and tried to think straight. What time had she left Aaron Trent's hotel? Was it one o'clock – or had it been after two?'

'Early afternoon,' she replied, and gabbled on so that no more searching questions could be asked. 'And then I drove to the motorway – the Ml, and joined it at junction twenty-nine, I think it was – near Chesterfield.' She racked her brain, trying to remember town names, and road numbers when she'd driven up here with Patric almost three months ago.

'Mrs Faulkner? Are you still there?'

Pain was washing over her in great waves. She drew in her breath and answered, 'Yes.'

'Where did you leave the motorway?'

'Leicester. Then I went across country and by-passed Huntingdon.'

'I see. I think we can be satisfied that you're no longer...'

'On your hit list?' Michelle asked, driven to sarcasm by the griping ache in her side.

Patric was on the phone again now. 'Michelle! I'm getting off the phone now. We need to contact other people.'

She drew in her breath again and willed the pain to go away. It was spreading though, spreading in a great aching, throbbing mass so that she couldn't even think straight about anything. 'Patric – I've got to go too. I really am feeling dreadful at the moment…'

'Then don't carry on driving,' he said. 'For Heavens' sake, Michelle – stay where you are. Call the motoring organisation. Tell them where you are…or ring for an ambulance…'

She leaned her head back against the head-rest on her seat and took short little panting breaths to try and ease the pain. Nothing seemed to be working against it now though, and she was getting scared. She heard a sound beside her, turned her head and looked straight into Tiffany's big solemn eyes. The baby yawned again, then gurgled and cooed.

'Michelle…'

She switched the phone off instantly, hoping he hadn't heard the sound that Tiffany had made. 'Oh, baby,' she muttered. 'What have I done? How can I look after you when I feel like this?'

At the flat in Rydale Tor the anxious little group held their breath.

'It was Tiff,' Cass cried. 'I know it was Tiff. It's the sound she makes when she wakes up. I *know* it was her!'

'Your suspicions were right then when you told me you'd seen a car that looked like the one Michelle Faulkner was driving when you spoke to her on the film set, driving away just after Tiffany vanished,' DCI Scholes said. 'Headquarters will have circulated the description and registration number by now. All counties will be on the lookout for her.'

'She can't possibly be in Suffolk,' Patric said. 'It would have taken her easily three hours to drive to Thetford from here – and Tiff's only been missing for just over half an hour. If she has Tiffany with her, she can't be out of

Derbyshire yet.' He turned to Erin Scholes, 'Don't you agree?'

'Entirely,' the woman said. 'There's something else, too. She lied about the motorway. There was an accident on the M1 at eleven o'clock today. Two southbound junctions are still closed.'

'Two junctions?' Patric asked. 'And they are?'

'Twenty-eight and twenty-nine. Two articulated lorries on their sides. All three lanes totally littered with oranges and reams of paper.'

Cass jumped up from the sofa, 'So Michelle couldn't have been on the motorway today?'

'Nowhere near the motorway,' Scholes said. 'North and South are ruled out.'

'And probably East as well,' Patric replied. 'She'd have had to cross over the motorway to go east, from Derbyshire – and she would have seen the diversion signs around Chesterfield.'

'South West, or North West then?' The inspector looked first at Patric, then at Cass. 'Can you think of a reason why she'd go that way?'

Patric shook his head. 'No reason at all.'

'Let's think of airports then. And boats.'

Cass was pacing up and down. 'Oh, no. No. She wouldn't try to take Tiffany abroad, surely?'

'Babies are the in-thing with her at the moment, Cass.' Patric was grim-faced. 'She can't take Tiffany out of the country though.'

'No.' The policewoman smiled. 'No. We can alert the ports. But she hasn't got a passport for the baby. No one would let her through without one.'

Patric stood by the window, thoughtfully gnawing on his lip. He turned into the body of the room again and said,

'She could take Tiff to Ireland and it would be hell's own job trying to find her there – in southern Ireland especially – parts of it are so remote. The English police would have no legal authority there, either.'

'Ireland!' Cass stared at him.

Scholes nodded. 'I'd already thought of that. And you're right. We'd have no jurisdiction in Ireland. The Irish Garda would take over. That could waste valuable time. The case might even end up before the courts.'

'What?' Patric was outraged.

Scholes turned to him. 'You are the child's father. Mrs Faulkner could well argue the point that she is its legal stepmother. I don't want things getting to that point. I do realise, though, like you, that parts of Southern Ireland are pretty remote.' She pulled out her phone and, at that point, Cass heard the downstairs door opening, and footsteps running up the stairs.

Then Greer burst into the room. 'I came,' she said, 'as soon as Mum gave me your message.' She started to cry and fumbled for a tissue in her pocket. 'I'd just popped out to buy Tiffany a little soft toy for while she was staying with us, and…'

DCI Scholes had been talking on the phone but she put it away now, turning around to say, 'Keep that soft toy. You could well need it. Headquarters have just told me there's been a sighting of Mrs Faulkner's car. It's heading towards Liverpool. Your guess was right, Mr Faulkner. Ireland it is. She means business. We're going to have to move fast!'

chapter twenty

Cass, Patric and Greer were alone in the large living-room of the flat now, and Greer was in the kitchen, tidying-up, and making yet more cups of strong tea.

Cass, her face drawn and pale, paced first to the window and then back again to the sofa, an said, 'I can't just sit here – waiting – and wondering.'

'The police said there was nothing we could do, love…'

'Patric – I know that we should stay put. But how do *you* feel about this? Can you just sit around – *waiting* – not knowing what's happening to Tiff…' her voice broke off. She shook her head vigorously. 'I'll never get through the night – I just can't stop thinking about her and wondering if she's frightened, or if Michelle's capable of looking after her, or if she's in any kind of danger.' She threw up her hands in despair and her voice took on a note of terror, 'Patric – what if Michelle hasn't got her, what if she didn't take her – and someone else did…'

He went over to her, drew her into his arms against the window, holding her tightly, whilst still looking down onto the wide promenade by the side of the river opposite. As they stood there, they both knew they were thinking the same thing – wishing with all their hearts that a car would draw up outside and someone would get out of it with their baby.

An hour had passed though since the police had left. It was nearly six o'clock.

DCI Erin Scholes had told them Tiffany's picture would

be shown on TV's East Midlands News programme, but they hadn't had the heart to switch the television set on. DCI Scholes had also suggested that if Tiffany hadn't been found by next day, it might help if they were both willing to go on television themselves and make an appeal for her to be returned.

Cass slid her arm round Patric's waist and looked down on the main street that was still busy with holiday-makers, and motorbikes were still roaring into Rydale Tor too.

Everything looked the same, but nothing was the same.

And still hanging over her was the memory of that meeting with Michelle – only a few hours ago that morning – and the things Michelle had told her about her marriage – and especially the bit about Patric being the father of the baby she was carrying…

She hadn't been able to tackle Patric about that yet, but it wasn't important any more. What was important was Tiffany – and her safe return.

Patric said, above her head, 'What do you want to do, Cass? For myself, I can't think of anything worse than this endless waiting.'

She looked up at him, wondering if he knew what Michelle had told her, and if he did know why, he didn't either confirm – or deny – that he and Michelle had become lovers again.

'What *can* we do? We know that Michelle's heading for Liverpool – and that the police have her under surveillance – whatever that might mean.'

'It means they've located her car – heading towards Liverpool, and they're following at a safe distance, and have alerted all the local forces in the area where she is. They won't lose her, Cass. They've got fast cars and heli-copters, but at the moment they don't want to arouse her suspicions so they're going about it all very quietly. It's the only way.'

'But if she somehow slips through…'

'She can't. She won't even be allowed aboard a ferry for Ireland.'

'She might panic if they refuse to take her…she might harm Tiff…'

'Cass!' He turned her in his arms, to face him. He took hold of her shoulders firmly and gripped them hard. 'Cass! Don't!' he said. 'Do you think I'm not going through hell myself, thinking "what-if" this and "what-if" that? I know Michelle better than most people, remember? I was married to her – and I know what she's capable of.'

'She killed Craig Andrews,' Cass cried wildly. 'You know she did – even though charges couldn't be upheld. We both know what she did.'

'I can't believe she'd hurt a helpless baby though…'

'I can! Patric – she hates me. This is her way of getting back at me.'

'She doesn't hate me though, Cass. She'd move Heaven and Earth to keep me with her. And Tiffany is my baby too. I just know she won't hurt Tiff.'

'I wish I thought so. But of course you know her better than I do.' There was a silent accusation in her eyes now though.

'What do you mean by that, Cass?' He was tense and his hands fell away from her.

'Michelle came to see me this morning. On the set – at Ashton. She told me…' She spun away from him, but he grabbed at her arm and pulled her back to face him. Tears gathered in Cass's eyes. '*OK* – she told me she was pregnant – and that you were the father of the child.'

'*What*?'

'I don't have to repeat it, Patric. She wants to hurt me. She tried this morning, and now this…'

He pulled her into his arms. 'Don't,' he whispered in a broken voice. 'Oh, Cass – don't tell me you believed her.'

'She can be very convincing – and if the baby isn't yours, then whose is it?'

'It's Aaron Trent's – if indeed she is pregnant,' he said wearily.

'Trent?' She stared at him, her eyes wide.

'A one-night stand – about a month ago. She'd tried to bribe me to sleep with her and give her a child…'

'Bribe you? What with?' Cass didn't know whether she ought to laugh or cry. It all sounded so ludicrous.

'The only thing she thought she could bribe me with – the promise of getting out of my life so I could be with you. But, Cass – I didn't touch her. I couldn't have slept with her or made love to her – and I told her so.'

Tears gathered in her eyes. 'Why didn't you tell me?'

'It wasn't pleasant. It wasn't something I could talk about. I was disgusted with her – and with myself too for ever having loved her, for ever thinking she was attractive.'

She leaned her head against his shoulder. 'I should never have believed her,' she said. 'Patric – I feel awful now, for even listening to her today…'

'There are more important things to worry about,' he said. 'And Cass – I know how you must have felt. I can just imagine the rage I would have been feeling if someone had told me you'd been sleeping with somebody else. Remember how jealous I've been of your friendship with Dillon Teasdale, for instance.'

'He's a good friend.' She looked up into his face. 'But there's never been anything else but friendship – there never will be for me with any other man but you.'

Patric drew in a deep breath and let out a sigh. 'I wish there was something we could do to help find Tiff,' he said. 'I feel so bloody helpless.'

'We don't have to sit here – helpless,' she said eagerly. 'Patric – why don't we go up to Liverpool ourselves – just so we're there when they apprehend Michelle? Thinking logically about it – Tiffany *must* be with her. Why else would Michelle spin that yarn to you and DCI Scholes about being in Suffolk when she was, in fact, on the way to Liverpool? She's hiding something. She has to be. And the only thing she can be trying to hide is the fact that she was the one who had snatched Tiffany.'

'I've been thinking that too,' he said. 'Shall we do it, Cass?'

She nodded. 'I'll tell Greer…' She was pulling away from him, racing across the room. 'Go and get the car started, Patric – I'll be downstairs in two minutes.'

He strode towards the door, ran down the stairs, and in two minutes flat, Cass had joined him in the car.

The baby was grizzly and bad-tempered. Michelle didn't know they could be like this. She wondered what was wrong with it, especially when the grizzling stopped and the yelling started.

She pulled the car into a side road off a roundabout and put the handbrake on, then turning to the baby beside her, muttering savagely, 'What on earth is wrong with you, you fractious and infuriating child?'

Tiffany's face was red and puffed up with crying. She stopped just long enough to glare at Michelle, then her bottom lip started to tremble again and a long wail rang out, causing Michelle to put her hands to her head. When the wailing just went on and on, she rested her head on the steering wheel, pressing her hands over her ears, and trying to somehow shut out the incessant noise.

She'd been reading 'baby' books just recently. They cried if they had wind, or if they were hungry or wet or…

'Disposables!' Michelle looked up at Tiffany again. 'Food! What on earth do you eat at your age?'

Tiffany continued to bawl as hard and as loud as she could.

Michelle placed the pink teddy in her hands and Tiff straightaway slung it back at her. And continued to howl.

Michelle started to drive again. They were on the outskirts of a small town. She ignored all signs for the ring road and went straight on ahead, and into the town centre, finding a little car park behind a supermarket, where she parked neatly, then turned to the baby again.

Tiffany was by now showing signs of exhaustion and had reverted to intermittent grizzling again.

Michelle realised she couldn't attract attention to her car by leaving Tiffany inside it while she shopped, so she unhitched the seat belt and carried the baby in the car-seat, then popped her in a deep shopping trolley while they went up and down the aisles.

She bought a pack of pink disposable nappies, not knowing – but just guessing at the size. She bought a carton of skimmed milk, a baby's feeding cup, a pack of picnic teaspoons, and a dozen jars of baby dinners and puddings.

Tiffany was being better behaved now as they went up and down the colourful aisles. She blinked at the bright lights overhead and reached out to people they passed.

Back in the car, and still in the car park before moving on, Michelle spoon-fed Tiffany one of the little jars of vegetable baby food, then poured some of the semi-skimmed milk into the baby's feeding cup and gave her that too.

Tiffany gurgled and burped her way through her 'meal' seeming bemused that she was having it in her car-seat and not her high-chair. She kept waving her hands and thumping them down on her knees, then looking surprised because they didn't make a rattly noise like her high-chair at home.

Michelle took some pain-killers because she still felt bad. The pain seemed to be everywhere now, and she began to worry that it wasn't something entirely natural about being pregnant that was wrong with her.

She started wondering too, what she had got herself into. It had been a spur of the moment thing – snatching the baby in Rydale Tor. It didn't seem like such a good idea now, but the police were on to her and Patric and Cass must be going wild with worry.

She sat and looked at Tiffany as the baby began nodding off to sleep after her meal. It seemed to be all they did – babies – Michelle thought, eating, sleeping, and making a hell of a racket when they didn't get what they wanted.

She wished she hadn't done what she'd done now, and her mind began to work overtime as she tried to decide what to do next.

It was nearly half-past seven, still light, but the sun wasn't shining any more. There were dark clouds coming up from the West. There'd be rain before morning.

Suddenly she felt incredibly weary. She needed to sleep. She wanted a nice hot bath, and then bed. Drowsily, she wondered whether Tiffany slept through the night – or would she want feeding again before morning?

She had to find somewhere to stay the night.

She put the car in motion again, and set off – heading again for Liverpool. Ireland was the only answer, but that would have to wait until tomorrow now.

There was an old school chum in Ireland. She hadn't seen Jennifer in years, but somebody in the village where Jen had lived would surely know if she was still there, in the little isolated cottage where Michelle had once been and spent a whole idyllic summer holiday.

But what did it matter anyway, whether Jennifer were there or not? There were always cottages for rent – and caravans…

First of all though, was the necessity of finding somewhere to stay the night!

chapter twenty-one

'We lost her! Cass – I'm sorry.' DCI Scholes, ringing through on Cass's mobile phone sounded more than sorry, she sounded angry too. 'Look – we're trying to pick up the trail again, but she shot off the main route to Liverpool and in a maze of streets, we lost her in a small town.'

'Oh, no!' Cass's fingers tightened round her phone as she sat staring out through the windscreen of Patric's car as rain drizzled down.

'What is it?' he asked alarmed, glancing at her.

'Michelle! They lost Michelle in some town near Liverpool.'

'*Hell…!*'

DCI Scholes was speaking again. 'We *will* find her. I promise you. But where are you, Cass? I tried ringing your flat but there was no reply.'

Firmly Cass said, 'We're on our way to Liverpool – Patric and I. We just couldn't sit around doing nothing.'

'I wish you had stayed put.' DCI Scholes' voice was sharp. 'There's nothing you can do up here. We've got a difficult job on. We can't risk anything going wrong – not when there's a baby involved. Some people do strange things on the spur of the moment, especially if they think they're trapped. And Mrs Faulkner doesn't come across as a very well-balanced sort of person. You really should have stayed at home.'

Cass had been holding the phone so that Patric too could hear what was being said. He yelled across at the phone now, 'No, DCI Scholes – Michelle is *not* well-balanced, believe me. That's why I want to be there when you find her. Michelle is childish, selfish, and will do anything to get her own way…'

'Patric – don't…' Cass pleaded. 'It doesn't help being so bitter.'

'Please,' Erin Scholes said. 'Please – turn right round and go back home.'

'No way,' Patric retorted grimly.

Cass shook her head. 'We can't do that. We want to be near Tiffany.'

'Your presence could antagonise Mrs Faulkner. Had you thought of that? Sometimes it's best if complete strangers…'

'I don't want Tiffany to be surrounded by complete strangers,' Cass told her firmly. 'I want to be the one to take my daughter in my arms – not someone in police uniform who's probably never handled a baby in their life.'

After another plea for them to return home – and another refusal, DCI Scholes rang off.

'Did she really think we'd go back?' Cass asked irately of Patric.

'Cass – she seems good at her job. Don't let it get at you.'

'But to lose Michelle's car…'

'It's easily done, love. It would have been at a busy time – when people were going home from work. Maybe Michelle had a reason for going into that town? Look on the positive side – maybe she was going to buy food for Tiffany? Knowing Michelle, she wouldn't have stopped to think of food, or nappies, or anything like that until she was forced to.'

'She could have come to Rydale Tor prepared though.'

Patric shook his head. 'I don't think so. I think it was a

spur-of-the-moment thing. She was there – and Tiff was there – and for a couple of seconds your back was turned. Michelle wouldn't stop to think of the consequences. It was like that night she killed Craig Andrews. She didn't stop to think – she just drove her car at him.'

Cass shuddered. 'Don't make such a comparison, Patric. I dread to think what she might do again.'

'She won't hurt Tiffany, Cass – I'm convinced of it. Tiffany is my flesh and blood, and Michelle has never attempted to harm me. I'm not scared of her, Cass. And I'm telling you – she won't harm the baby. She's far more likely to try and pass Tiffany off as her own child.'

'I hope you're right.' Rain was pelting down on the windscreen now. 'Oh, Patric – I hope and pray that you're right.'

DCI Scholes rang them again when they were on the outskirts of Liverpool.

'Have you found her? Is there any news of Tiffany?' Cass was churning up inside by now.

'We know she stopped off at a supermarket and bought baby food and other items. We also know she spoon-fed the baby in the car before setting off again. Somebody saw her.'

Cass closed her eyes and said a silent prayer. 'And then?' she asked. 'Have you traced her again?'

'We don't think she's got as far as Liverpool. It's my guess she's gone somewhere for the night.'

'Somewhere? But where?' Cass looked worriedly at Patric.

He slowed the car as they were coming up to a traffic island.

'As near as we can make out, she must be in the Warrington, or even the St Helen's area. Warrington was near where she made that call on the supermarket more than an hour ago now. We've got a check on all roads into Liverpool from that direction however, and Mrs Faulkner's car hasn't been spotted yet.'

Patric took a turn off the island, and pulled to a halt at the side of the less busy road. 'Now what?'

Feeling at a loss herself, Cass asked Erin Scholes, 'What do you suggest we do now then?'

'We're checking hotels and hospitals,' DCI Scholes said.

Cass's heart missed a beat. 'Hospitals?'

'Just as a precaution.'

'Oh, God!' Cass swallowed painfully, unable to speak for a second or two. Did they really think Michelle was dangerous, she wondered? Dangerous to Tiffany? Would she harm the baby?

'I have a suggestion to make.' Erin Scholes was speaking again. 'Could you ask Mr Faulkner to try and telephone his ex-wife, without giving away the fact that we believe she's got the child with her?'

'Patric's tried to ring Michelle several times,' Cass said. 'She's turned her phone off.'

'Just ask him to keep trying. It might speed things up. She might drop a hint as to where she is – if she doesn't persist in the lie that she's gone home to Suffolk.'

Cass handed Patric the phone. Patric said, 'I've tried ringing the house in Suffolk. There's no one there.'

'We must assume then that Mrs Faulkner *is* the kidnapper.' There was a moment's silence and then DCI Scholes said, 'I'd feel better if you were here with us.' She gave the address of a police station in the suburbs of Liverpool. 'Can you make your way there? As you've come this far, I think we might as well all try and work together.'

Rain had set in with a vengeance. In the police station office though it was warm and dry. Cass's thoughts were on Tiffany all the time. Was *she* warm, was *she* dry? Could Michelle have dumped her somewhere? Had there been an accident?

It was better being at the heart of things though. They were there as DCI Scholes and her colleagues were besieged with phone calls from people who had seen Tiff's picture on television.

'We have to sift through the calls, she told them. 'Some of them just can't be the right baby these people have seen. We've had calls from as far away as Manchester and York, saying there's been a sighting of Tiffany with a dark woman at two o'clock this afternoon, but Tiffany was at home with you then, Cass.'

'But where can Michelle have vanished to?' Patric was irate. 'Surely you just couldn't have 'lost' her?'

'I've got people out checking hotels and guest houses,' Erin Scholes said. 'They've been issued with photographs of Tiffany – a pity we don't have a picture of Mrs Faulkner though. We're having to make-do with a physical description only there.'

'And the hospitals?' Patric put into words what Cass had been avoiding.

'Good news there. No road traffic accidents involving women with young children. No abandoned babies! They're still together, it seems – Mrs Faulkner and Tiffany.'

'We must be able to *do* something though,' Cass cried.

Erin Scholes said, 'You're tired. There's a back room.' She nodded beyond the door. 'It's really an old cell, but there's a bunk in there. You should go and get some rest. I'll be here to wake you the minute we receive any news.'

Cass swayed on her feet. Patric was there to put an arm round her. 'Come on. You're totally exhausted.'

She turned to him. 'I couldn't sleep. I just couldn't, Patric.'

'There's an armchair.' Erin Scholes shrugged. 'Please – let my sergeant show you the room. You're wearing yourselves out with worry – and tomorrow – you may need your strength because it's then that Mrs Faulkner is going to try and get to Ireland. But we'll be ready for her. It's going to be a tough day.'

Worn down by the argument, Cass agreed to try and sleep in the cell. She and Patric were led away to the back of the building and left alone there.

She cried softly in his arms, repeating and repeating that she knew she would never see her baby again.

Patric tried to allay her fears. He lay down on the bunk, holding her close.

It was a long night and neither of them slept.

They sipped mugs of hot tea at seven next morning. Cass felt as if she'd been battered and bruised, she was so tired. She could only think of Tiffany and, with every minute that passed, it seemed to her as if her baby was moving further and further away from her.

DCI Scholes hurried in through the open cell door.

'A possible lead. The helicopter's spotted what looks like an abandoned car fitting the description of…'

Patric and Cass leapt to their feet and raced out after Erin Scholes. They were bundled into the back of a police car, even though Patric said he could take his own car.

Sirens blaring, they weaved through morning traffic until they were out on an open road with sparse woodland on either side of them.

Two more police cars were keeping up with them.

Ahead, Cass saw a helicopter hovering over a belt of

trees. As they drew near, a paramedic ambulance came from the opposite direction and turned off onto a track leading into the trees.

'Up there.' DCI Scholes sat forward in her seat in the front of the car. The driver put his foot down. The speedometer crept up and up.

They bumped over rough ground, following the rear of the ambulance. Cass and Patric were leaning forward too now, staring at a spot just beyond where the ambulance had come to a standstill and two paramedics had jumped out.

'It's Michelle's car.' Patric's voice was harsh with concern. 'Oh my God.'

DCI Scholes turned round in her seat. 'Stay here!'

Cass shook her head wildly from side-to-side, already out of her seat belt and scrambling to open the door.

She was out and running towards the car and ambulance, both of which were in a small clearing, and Patric was hot on her heels.

She reached the car first. All its door were wide open. Michelle was in the front seat – the driver's seat. She was staring straight ahead through the windscreen.

Cass had no time for Michelle. She was screaming for Tiffany and throwing herself in the back door of the car, searching, searching for some sign of the baby, but there was none.

She was out of the car then, racing round the back, trying to open the boot and banging and banging her hands on it in frustration.

They'd got Michelle out of the car now. On the ground. Her eyes were tightly closed. Cass ran round to her still screaming, 'What have you done with my baby... what have you done with my baby...'

Somebody had the car boot open now, she heard it opening. She whirled round, but DCI Scholes was shaking her head. 'No sign of the child.'

Cass was sobbing and Patric was holding her tightly in his arms. His face was grim, his lips set in a thin, tight line.

The paramedics had Michelle on a stretcher now. There was a blanket over her, covering her whole body.

Cass pulled away from Patric and raced round to that side of the car. There was blood on the ground. Inside the car too, the seat was stained red.

Wide-eyed, she stared at Erin Scholes. Behind the Detective Inspector the paramedics were putting the stretcher in the ambulance.

She raced away again, this time to the ambulance. 'Ask her,' she yelled at the two paramedics. 'For God's sake ask her where my baby is?'

They looked beyond her to where Patric was running across the clearing to them.

'It's no use,' he said, coming up behind her and holding onto her shoulders.

She leaned back against him, all fight gone out of her.

'She's unconscious, isn't she?' She half turned her head towards Patric.

'Michelle? Yes,' he said.

'And my baby?'

'Not here,' he said. 'Tiffany certainly isn't here, Cass.'

'Then where is she?' she cried with stark terror in her voice, and turning round fully now to face him.

He raised his hands helplessly. 'I don't know, Cass. I just don't know.'

chapter twenty-two

DCI Erin Scholes was half in, half out of the front of Michelle's car when suddenly she turned her head and shouted for Patric.

Grasping hold of Cass's hand, Patric ran over to the car.

Erin Scholes was out of the car now, holding up an envelope. 'I found this – on the dashboard. It has your name on it.'

Patric had turned pale. 'A suicide note?' he asked. Then he shook his head. 'No. I can't believe that – not of Michelle.'

'Open it. Please.' Erin Scholes was still holding onto the envelope, her hand stretched out towards him. 'Please,' she insisted. 'If you don't, then I will. A child's life might be at stake here.'

'Tiffany…' Cass beside him whispered the name.

Patric took the envelope and ripped it open, read what was written and then handed it back to the Detective Inspector.

'We've got to get back – to that place she mentions,' he stated, and his hands, Cass noted, were shaking visibly. 'I remember,' he said, concentrating, 'I remember driving through a town of that name last night…'

'And the hotel? This note gives the precise location – overlooking a park on the outskirts of the town, the Park Hotel. Come along. Hurry now. My driver will know it.'

The note was handed to Cass, who read through it quickly and then held it close to her chest. 'Can we phone the place…?' She looked up to see Erin Scholes already dialling a number on her phone.

They all piled into the police car. DCI Scholes was still talking on the phone, then turned around to Cass, a big beaming smile on her face as the car shot off, and said, 'She's there. Unharmed. They've found her.'

They raced across the car park and burst into the hotel through the wide, glazed doors.

Erin Scholes followed at a more leisurely pace, but caught them up in the foyer just as Tiffany was being handed over to Cass.

Cass was trembling all over, and kissing the baby's face, her hands, her hair, and hugging her close and rocking her as if she'd never let her go again.

Patric said, 'Let me have her. You're exhausted. Absolutely whacked.' He turned to the hotel receptionist and all the other staff who had gathered round them and who, it seemed, had been lavishing Tiffany with attention ever since they'd found her, curled up asleep, safe and well in the room that Michelle had booked into, the night before.

'I want to thank you – thank you all,' he said emotionally. 'For looking after my baby – for finding her – for keeping her safe.'

They found out after enquiries had been made that Michelle obviously hadn't stayed there long – just long enough to make sure the baby was clean and dry, and was safely bedded down for the night in the high-sided cot beside the bed. One of the hotel porters had seen her leaving the car park around eleven the night before. He hadn't been there when she arrived so didn't know about the baby.

There were traces of blood in the bathroom, indicating that Michelle was perhaps having a miscarriage, DCI

Scholes told them later.

'It wasn't attemted suicide then?' Patric seemed relieved that Michelle hadn't been driven to take her own life.

Back at the police station, Scholes had a report from the hospital where Michelle had been taken.

Calmly, Erin Scholes told them, 'The initial examination they've done on her shows there was no baby. She had an ulcer and it ruptured. She's lucky to be alive.'

'She'll be OK, though?' Patric asked.

Scholes nodded her head. 'She'll be fine. It's a common occurrence though, and with medical intervention, there's little risk to the patient – providing help is sought – which in Michelle's case, sadly, it wasn't.'

'She wanted a baby so badly,' Patric said. 'She explains that in the letter – that she's feeling rough and has started to bleed. That's why she left Tiffany at the hotel, so that Tiffany wouldn't be scared if she heard any noise, or was disturbed by strangers coming and taking Michelle away in the night.'

Cass, with tears in her eyes said, 'I didn't think she thought enough of Tiffany to do that. I didn't think she cared about her – or anyone, except herself.'

'Tiffany's *my* baby, Cass,' Patric said gently. 'I told you that Michelle wouldn't hurt her.'

'It's sad that your wife isn't having the baby she thought she was expecting,' Erin Scholes said.

Patric lifted his head and looked at the woman. 'Michelle wasn't my wife,' he explained. 'We were divorced eighteen months ago. The baby she hoped for wasn't mine. I do have a phone call to make though. The man who thought he was the father of the child has a right to know what's happened.'

Cass sat beside Patric in his car, with Tiffany asleep in her car-chair on the back seat while he rang Aaron Trent and told him the tragic news about Michelle and the baby.

Afterwards, Trent asked to speak to 'Sandie'

Cass felt drained, but took the phone from Patric.

'Sandie-baby, are you OK? We all of us here heard what had happened. Saw Tiffany's picture on the television last night. It's been hell, Sandie, wondering how you were coping.'

'I'm OK, Aaron.' Cass managed a little laugh. 'I'd almost forgotten my other name – Sandie – though.'

'A blast from the past, as they say, sweetheart.' Trent seemed not to know what else to say.

'Was it only yesterday that was the "past",' she murmured.

'Sandie – I'm gutted, real gutted that I was unwittingly the cause of Michelle's behaviour.'

'You mustn't blame yourself…' Only minutes ago, Patric had said the same thing to Trent as she'd listened. She knew he would be taking it hard though.

'A one-night stand, Sandie-baby – sends her over the top!' She heard the catch in his voice, the half-sob that came to her over the miles.

She didn't know what to say.

His voice steadied. 'You have Tiffany safe and well though?'

'Yes.' She looked at Patric and squeezed his hand. 'Michelle took good care of her for the little while she had her.'

'I'm glad, baby. Real glad about that.'

She turned to Patric when the phone call was over. 'Can we go home now?'

He nodded slowly. 'I'll have to come back, of course.

There'll probably be an enquiry, and there are arrangements to make about Michelle…'

'I'm sorry it had to end like this.' She *was* sorry. Michelle had been in many ways an evil woman, but nobody deserved the terribly sad fate which had just befallen her.

'So am I' Patric sounded tense. 'Michelle would have cared for Tiffany – there's no doubt about that. But she would have also tried to manipulate the poor child. Just as she did everyone with whom she came into contact.'

'I wonder if a baby would have made any difference to your marriage – if she'd had a child all those years ago,' she said.

Patric shook his head. 'The truth is that she was the one who never wanted kids. She was scared of losing her figure, her looks…'

He leaned forward and kissed Cass warmly and passionately on the lips. In the back of the car, baby Tiffany grunted in her sleep and settled herself into a more comfortable position.

'We have Tiffany back. We have her to think of now – as well as ourselves,' he said at last. 'Nothing can wipe out the past. Nothing can change what Michelle did. We have the chance to make a new start now, Cass.'

She leaned her head back and closed her eyes. She felt Patric pulling the seat belt over her shoulder and fastening it in position. She heard him laugh.

She opened her eyes and looked at him, loving him for his gentleness, his strength – and his weaknesses too. Each of them had weaknesses which they'd have to work at. Everyone did. There never was and never had been the perfect partnership.

It was a time for forgiveness though. Michelle couldn't hurt them now.

Grief would be brief and, in time, Michelle's part in their lives would fade away and be forgotten like an echo.

But destiny was giving them a second chance – a chance to repair the past and make a new start – and for that she was grateful.

She looked at Patric and he looked at her. The tension was relaxing in his face. She smiled across at him, and in the back seat baby Tiffany gave a big yawn.

Patric started up the car and said, 'Time to go home, I think.'

Romance at its best from Heartline Books™

We're sure that you've enjoyed the latest selection of titles from Heartline. We can offer you even more new novels by our talented authors over the coming months. Heartline will be bringing you stories with a dash of mystery, some which are tinged with humour and others highlighting the passion and pain of love lost and re-discovered. Our unique and eye-catching covers will capture backdrops which include the glamorous, exotic desert, an idyllic watermill in the English countryside and the charm of a traditional bookshop.

Whatever the setting, you can be sure that our heroes and heroines will be people you will care about and want to spend time with. Authors we shall be featuring will include Angela Drake, Harriet Wilson and Clare Tyler, while each month we will do our best to bring you an author making her sparkling debut in the world of romantic fiction.

If you've enjoyed these books why not tell all your friends and relatives that they, too, can start a new romance with Heartline Books today, by applying for their own, **ABSOLUTELY FREE**, copy of Natalie Fox's LOVE IS FOREVER. To obtain their free book, they can:

- visit our website: www.heartlinebooks.com
- *or* telephone the Heartline Hotline on 0845 6000504
- *or* enter their details on the form below, tear it off and send it to:
  Heartline Books,
  FREEPOST LON 16243, Swindon, SN2 8LA

And, like you, they can discover the joys of subscribing to Heartline Books, including:

♥ A wide range of quality romantic fiction delivered to their door each month

♥ A monthly newsletter packed with special offers, competitions, celebrity interviews and other exciting features

♥ A bright, fresh, new website created just for our readers

Please send me my free copy of *Love is Forever*:

Name (IN BLOCK CAPITALS)

_____

Address (IN BLOCK CAPITALS)

_____

_____

_____

_____ Postcode _____

If you do not wish to receive selected offers
from other companies, please tick the box ☐

If we do not hear from you within the next ten days, we will be sending you four
exciting new romantic novels at a price of £3.99 each, plus £1 p&p. Thereafter,
each time you buy our books, we will send you a further pack of four titles.

Heartline Books...

Romance at its best ™